THE LONG ISLAND PROJECT

A Time Travel Odyssey

Russell F. Moran

The Long Island Project
A Time Travel Odyssey

Coddington Press

Copyright © 2020 by Russell F. Moran

www.morancom.com

Printed in the United States of America

ISBN-978-1-7338872-3-6

Covers and text design by LuAnn T. Palazzo
www.PalazzoDM.com

DEDICATION

This book is dedicated to the men and women police detectives.

ACKNOWLEDGEMENTS

As always, I thank my wife, Lynda, for her attentive reading, rereading, and editing of my many drafts, and for laughing at my jokes. Lynda is to me as Bobbie is to Bob. I also thank my friend and editor, John White, for his keen editorial eye. I thank LuAnn T. Palazzo for her expert interior and cover designs. I also thank Dennis Ciano, retired NYPD homicide detective, for his expert advice. And I especially thank my readers, many of whom are a constant source of inspiration and encouragement for me.

AUTHOR'S NOTE

The Long Island Project is Book 3 in the *Puzzles* Series, and a continuation of the adventures of detectives Bob and Bobbie. Bob and Bobbie are two of my favorite characters, and I think of them as old friends. As I wrote this book, we took a lot of adventures together. I hope you will see them that way too.

You will find a **Cast of Characters** after the last chapter of the book. It can be frustrating to come across a character on page 150, that you first met on page 20, especially if you've put the book down for a few days. I've seen this done in Russian literature, and I happily add a cast of characters to *The Long Island Project* as well as my other novels.

CHAPTER 1

Bobbie Nelson

Alexa, how's traffic on the Long Island Expressway?"

"The traffic is extremely light because of the quarantine."

What? Did she say quarantine? I couldn't believe what I just heard from our Echo device. Bob walked up next to me, looking as freaked out as I felt.

Bob and I love our Alexa Echo device. It's a small cylinder that sits in the corner of a room. You activate it by saying the word "Alexa." That connects you to a vast Internet database in the cloud. You can ask it all kinds of questions or give it commands, such as "Alexa, turn on the patio lights," or "Alexa what is the current time in Belgrade," or "Alexa what is the score of the Giants-Dolphins game?" In her pleasant woman's voice, she'll not only give you the score but will fill in some details, such as "The Giants won by three points with a field goal kicked by Aldrick Rosas in the last 20 seconds."

It's easy to fall in love with Alexa, but after what she just said I think I hate her.

"Alexa, please explain the Long Island quarantine and when it started," Bob said.

Alexa continued, "The armed quarantine began this morning at 6 a.m. Eastern Time. There is no way on or off Long Island. None of my resources tell me anything further about the situation."

We walked into the kitchen where our adopted little two-year-old girl, Tilly, sat at the table. Jane, Tilly's governess, stood there with Steve Rankin, her fiancé. Jane, and usually Steve, accompany Bob and me when we visit our vacation home in East Hampton. We think of Jane and Steve as part of our family. They stared at the TV without saying a word. Obviously, they heard the news that Bob and I just heard from Alexa—the Long Island quarantine.

"Am I dreaming this?" Jane said, her eyes peeled to the TV as she poured coffee into her orange juice.

"Who the hell would quarantine Long Island? And why?" I said with the sinking feeling that there was no answer to my question.

"Alexa, who is responsible for the quarantine of Long Island?" I asked.

"I do not have the resources to comment on who is behind this action," Alexa said in one of her rare statements that lacks details.

"The guy on the news gave no specifics," Jane said, "just that Long Island is under strict quarantine until further notice. Let's flip some channels and catch the latest."

"Just to give you folks an update," the TV reporter said, "yes, Long Island is under strict and total quarantine until further notice. No one is allowed on or off the island."

The guy said it calmly and actually wore a smile—a friggin smile as he announced a bizarre quarantine of Long Island.

"We haven't been able to find a reason for this measure," the reporter continued, "but we have been told that the quarantine will be strictly enforced—by arrest and imprisonment if the order is disobeyed."

"I don't recognize that guy," Jane said, staring wide-eyed at the TV. "He must be new."

We waited for the next reporter to speak. A woman named Gloria Jensen, whom we had never seen before, calmly delivered a report concerning the grape harvest from East End vineyards. What? Long Island is under armed quarantine and she's talking about fucking crop yields? The next reporter, whom we had never seen or heard of, recounted a liquor store burglary in Bay Shore. Then came another stranger who discussed a hit and run accident in Medford. The next reporter talked about the upcoming Strawberry Festival in Mattituck. Holy shit. Long Island is under lockdown, and these clowns are talking about crop yields, burglaries, car accidents, and a Strawberry Festival? I felt a knot in my stomach. The four of us just stared at each other. We decided to continue watching the local Long Island TV network. Twenty-five minutes went by with no further mention of the quarantine. We decided to channel surf to see what the other networks had to say about this incredible story. We turned to *ABC, CBS, CNN, Fox* and *NBC*. All we saw were reporters we had never seen before. It's as if there was a massive personnel turnover, and all the networks replaced their reporters with fresh talent, and I wasn't sure how talented they were. We expected to see constant reports of the Long Island quarantine. But no. Every few minutes a reporter would mention the Long Island quarantine with about as much intensity as announcing the latest weather report.

Bob and I have been around the block a few times as detectives, and I think we're damn good cops. An article about us in *The New York Times* used a term that Bob Lawton and Bobbie Nelson have become famous for—the BBs. Our boss and friend, NYPD Commissioner Ralph Norquist always heaps praise on us, and even says that we're NYPD *royalty*. Well, that's nice, but after the shit we just heard on TV, neither of us felt much like royalty. Detectives are paid to figure out complicated stuff, assemble evidence, to look for clues, and solve puzzles. But we're clueless—the BBs are totally fucking clueless.

Jane, who is a terrific cook as well as a wonderful governess, put out a heaping bowl of scrambled eggs accompanied by a platter of bacon and sausages. It smelled delicious, but none of us felt hungry.

"Maybe it's some sort of health emergency," Steve said. "It can't be a nuclear accident because the Shoreham Nuclear Power plant was decommissioned in 1989 and that was the only nuclear reactor on Long Island. Maybe it's a flu epidemic."

Truth was, none of us had any idea what was going on, and the TV reporters weren't any help.

———————

We were staying the weekend at our house in East Hampton along with Jane, Steve, and our little Tilly. Buying the house was one of the best moves we ever made. We love it there. The neighborhood is beautiful, with one exquisite house after another. I always think of myself as a kid from Queens, and never gave opulence much thought. But we had just received our first royalty check from our book *Detectiving*. It was $20,000, even though we had already received a $15 million advance. Bob's average royalty check from his first novel, *An Army of Blue*, is also a best seller, and brings in $5,000 per month. And, God knows, with the huge amount of overtime Bob and I put in, our combined salaries are over $300,000. So, we've got a few bucks. Hey, life's too short—why not live it up a little?

I remember the day Lorie Fitzgerald, a real estate broker, showed us the house. She was highly recommended by our boss, NYPD Commissioner Ralph Norquist. Ralph owned a vacation home near ours. As she drove us around, Lorie didn't point the house out to us, but drove by it a couple of times, faking that she was lost. She definitely had a flair for the dramatic. When she finally pulled into the driveway, Bob and I both gasped. It was the house we kept nudging each other about as we drove around. It was two stories high and had a long, elegant, sloping roof. The shingling was classic New England, but it was obvious that the house was almost new. Next to the swimming pool was a tastefully designed pool house that matched the lines of the home. We walked through the front door into a huge hallway with a vaulted ceiling over which was a large roof skylight. I couldn't recall ever seeing such a spectacular entrance hallway. We walked around the first floor.

"Knowing you guys, you will love this," she said as she opened a door to a gymnasium—it was too large to be called a gym. It looked like a commercial exercise club with every type of equipment you can imagine. Four large TV screens adorned the walls. Bob and I like to watch TV as we work out, and in this place we'd have a view from every piece of equipment. About 50 feet from the gym was what can best be described as a playroom. It boasted a huge pool table, a ping pong table, and three card tables. The wall panels were made of sumptuous cherry wood.

We then walked into the kitchen/dining area. The combined space was so large we could host a party of 75 without ever leaving the room. From the glass doors by the dining area we could see Georgica Pond, a lovely view to dine in front of. Naturally, it had every type of appliance imaginable, including some things I had no idea what they were for. Maybe I'll learn to cook, I thought as we walked around the kitchen. Let's not get carried away. God gave us restaurants for a reason. Bob tells me I make great reservations.

Each of the eight bedrooms was *en suite,* with an elegant modern full bath included. There was also a master bedroom suite on the first floor, which will probably come in handy if Bob and I grow old in this place. The master suite upstairs took our breaths away, with its lovely view of Georgica Pond beyond the second-floor deck. It was almost all glass, with windows and sliding doors leading onto the deck. In the bathroom was a hot tub. Bob and I *love* hot tubs. A small kitchenette was the perfect spot to make coffee to sip on the deck and take in the view of the water. In the hallway outside the master suite was a large closet. Lorie opened the door and we saw that the closet was a sauna. *A sauna?* I'm just a cop who grew up in Queens, and I couldn't wrap my mind around the idea of a sauna right near our bedroom.

The furniture was beautiful. Obviously, the owners have exquisite taste.

"Hey, Lorie, we don't have enough furniture to fill up one room in this place," I said, laughing.

"Oh, I forgot to tell you, Bobbie, the house comes fully furnished, including the gym."

Wow, seven million was starting to look like a bargain. And the fun thing to contemplate was that we could afford it.

Lorie took us to another room on the first floor near the gym.

"Hey, Bob, I think this should be our office. There's the perfect spot for facing desks."

"Oh, I read about that in your detective book," Lorie said. "So, detectives like to face each other so they can communicate about their cases. Do you also write books together that way?"

"Yes, we do," I said, not mentioning that we often come up with book ideas while making love. We enjoy multi-tasking.

We took one more trip through the house to see if we missed anything.

"So why don't I let you two chat while I go outside." Lorie seemed to know that sometimes the best pressure is *no* pressure.

Bob and I looked at each other and had one of our non-verbal conversations.

"Do you think there is any wiggle room in the price?" I asked before Lorie walked out. She gave me the answer I expected.

"I'll be honest with you guys; this house is priced to sell at seven million. It hasn't formally gone on the market yet. When it does, I expect a bidding war and a sale on the first day."

"We'll take it," Bob and I both said.

Case closed.

———

It's a good thing we love our East Hampton house, because the news reports about the goddam quarantine indicate that we'll be staying here for quite a while. Being a Sunday, we planned to head back to our condo in Manhattan. We had recently performed a major renovation after our next-door tenant moved out. We doubled the size of the place and it's now a 3,000 square foot beauty with four complete bedroom suites. Bob had bought the entire building of eight units two years ago before we got married. Bob was already a best-selling author of a novel entitled *An Army of Blue – Stories of New York City Cops*. God bless book royalties. I wondered if we'd ever see our Manhattan apartment again. I was still trying to come to grips with the fact that Long Island is quarantined.

"Bobbie, I think it's time to make some phone calls. Reporters in one of the hottest news markets in the country don't seem to give a rat's ass about this incredible story. I'm going to call Ralph Norquist. I'm sure the Commissioner of the NYPD has got a handle on this insanity."

———————

"Commissioner Norquist's office, Pamela Jackson speaking, may I help you?"

Neither Bob nor I ever heard of a Pamela Jackson—and she's answering the commissioner's phone. Surprises were starting to pile up like logs.

"This is Detective Bobbie Nelson, may I please speak to the commissioner?"

"I'm sorry, Detective, but Commissioner Norquist isn't here today."

That's weird. We knew that Ralph was working on Sunday to prepare for a major meeting the next day, a meeting that we were scheduled to attend.

"May I speak to Margie Nathan, the commissioner's assistant?" Bob said, looking pissed off.

"She isn't here either. I have no idea when she'll return. May I help you with anything?"

"Yes, Pamela, can you tell me and my partner anything about this crazy quarantine of Long Island?"

"I really don't have much to tell you. I'm sure the problem will go away soon."

"Pamela, do you know me? Do you know my partner and husband Bob Lawton?"

"I'm afraid we haven't met."

"Pamela, are you new? Neither Bob nor I recognize your name."

"Today is my first day on the job. I really must be going. A pleasure speaking to you, Detective."

She hung up before I could say another word.

"Let's call Ralph's cellphone, honey. This is urgent and I'm sure he won't mind."

Bob and I are two of very few people who have the commissioner's secure cellphone number. We only use if for emergencies and this was beginning to look like an emergency.

After one ring we got the message: "The number you are calling is not in service at this time."

I looked at Bob and we both said, "What the fuck?" We agreed that we need to expand our vocabulary because we've both said, "What the fuck," about 20 times each this morning. But "what the fuck" seemed somehow appropriate for this bizarre crap we're going through. Lucky, our French Bulldog puppy, barked at the word "fuck," as Jane had trained him. He also barks at the word "shit." We try to keep our language cussword free when around Tilly, and Jane appointed herself project manager for the task. We don't want Tilly to grow up sounding like a cop.

"You know who's next, Bobbie."

"I agree, let's call him."

Bob and I are used to completing each other's sentences and communication with just a word, a phrase, or a glance. The word close doesn't begin to describe the relationship between Bob and me. Bob once said that sometimes the two of us disappear and show up as one person. I recalled the fabulous sex we had just a few hours ago, and part of me wanted to grab Bob's hand and go back to bed and rid our minds of this insanity.

I dialed the office of the Director of the Central Intelligence Agency, Gamal Akhbar, aka Charles Atkins, but everybody calls him Buster. We've worked closely with him on a number of cases and we're good friends. Unlike most CIA directors, Buster came up through the ranks as an agent, a seasoned spy.

"Office of the Director, this is Marilyn Swanson, may I help you?"

"Is Barbara Peters there?" I said, referring to Buster's long-time aide.

"No, Ms. Peters will be gone for an indeterminate amount of time."

Bob and I whispered yet another "what the fuck." I was beginning to feel like an extra in a science fiction movie.

"Okay, please put me through to Buster, this is Detective Bobbie Nelson. He knows me well."

"The Director isn't here, and I have no idea when he'll return. May I take a message?"

Buster has a well-earned reputation as a problem solver, and he always makes sure that he's available. When he was a field agent, people referred to him as a *super spook*. But where the hell can he be?

"Yes, please ask him to call me right away, It's urgent."

"May I ask the nature of the urgency, Detective?"

"The quarantine of Long Island."

"I hadn't heard about that. I'm sure the director will get back to you." She hung up.

"Did you guys catch that?" I said. "The woman from the CIA claimed that she hadn't heard about the quarantine of Long Island. Do you realize how many fucking robots we've spoken to in the past few minutes?" Lucky barked and Jane gave him a treat for snapping at my cussword. "I'll try Buster's cellphone. He always said not to hesitate to use it if there's something urgent, and I sure as hell think this is urgent."

"The number you are calling is not in service at this time."

My impatience was starting to be replaced with fear. The look on his face told me that Bob was feeling the same thing—and Bob never shows fear. He may feel it, I'm sure, but he never shows it.

"I think our next call should be to the White House."

"Are you serious, Bobbie?"

"Why not? First Lady Meg Fenton is also the president's new chief of staff. She's a big fan of ours."

I called the White House, introduced myself and asked to speak to the First Lady. Not to my surprise, I didn't recognize the person who picked up the phone. She told me the First Lady would not be taking any calls for the near future. I asked her to give Meg Fenton a message. The woman let out a chuckle and a sigh, as if she knew the message would never get through.

Our next call was to Rudy Jenkins, the NYPD Chief of Detectives. Rudy is our immediate boss, although Commissioner Ralph likes to work directly with Bob and me.

"Detective Jenkins office, this is Mary Blakely, may I help you?"

Bob and I stared at each other. Neither of us ever heard of Mary Blakely. She told us that Detective Jenkins would be out of the office for the near future. The near future? I then asked to speak to Phil Simonetti, Rudy's long-time aide, but was told that he was inaccessible.

"Hey, Bob, we're the best detectives on the street, and we can't seem to figure this crap out. Let's review what's happening. We called Ralph Norquist—not in. Then we called Buster at the CIA—not in either. And both Ralph's and Buster's cellphones are disconnected. And we couldn't get through to Rudy Jenkins either. We couldn't even get through to the First Lady. But the killer is this: We didn't recognize any of the people we spoke to. I feel like we're watching a movie about alternative reality."

"This isn't a bunch of coincidences, Bobbie. Hell, we both agree that coincidences are rare. Somebody is in charge of this. Somebody is making this happen."

"I agree, Bob. But who?"

Jane and Steve looked just as stunned as Bob and me. We think of Jane as a friend and sister, not just an employee. Jane is 28 years old, has a beautiful figure and a cute face that's framed by her natural cascade of blond curls. Jane was orphaned at age six and grew up in foster homes. She once told us that we're the family she never had. I still get choked up when I remember her saying that. I think that gives her a special love for our little Tilly, an orphan herself. Bob and I adopted Tilly six months ago. Her parents were killed by a robber. Bob and I were assigned to the case. It was one of the most gruesome crime scenes I ever investigated. Tilly's parents were lying dead on the living room floor in a pool of blood. I walked over to a bassinette and looked in. There was the most beautiful little girl I had ever seen. I stood there holding my gun and tried to calm the baby. Then I heard—and felt— a gunshot. I spent the next six weeks hospitalized in a semi-comatose state from a bullet wound to the base of my skull. Bob saved my life by shooting the man who shot me before he could get off another round. I kept dreaming about the adorable little girl. When I came out of my coma, I realized that it wasn't a dream—it really happened. I checked with Child Protective Services and discovered that the little girl was still at the agency, having not been adopted yet. I talked to Bob about her nonstop. "That baby needs a loving home," I told Bob. I will never forget his words.

"Then why don't we give her one," Bob said. "I can't imagine a more loving home than ours. Let's adopt her."

That's Bob. He's got a heart bigger than an ocean. I think I love Bob more than life itself. Yes, let's adopt her! So, we did, and nicknamed her Tilly, short for Tillary, her legal name. A few weeks later, Bob rescued an adorable little French Bulldog puppy, which Tilly named Lucky. Our happy family was growing.

"Steve and I would love to go for a swim in the pool, if only to get our minds off this weirdness."

"Take all the time you want," I said. "None of us are going anywhere soon. Bob and I are putting on our detective hats and we'll head into town for an early lunch to see if we can find out more about this insane quarantine."

CHAPTER 2

Bob

Bobbie and I have been through a lot together, and most of it has been good—make that great. Two years ago, Bobbie was recruited by NYPD Police Commissioner Ralph Norquist from her job as a police detective in Chicago. In an almost unheard-of move, the NYC mayor sent Norquist on a country-wide tour to recruit cops, mainly detectives, from other police departments. The NYPD was soaked in scandal at the time with countless reports of cops taking bribes. Mayor Paxton basically said, "Screw it, I've got a city to run and I don't give a damn about the union contracts." Bobbie accepted his offer and moved to New York City, the place where she grew up. She was probably the most famous detective in the country. She appeared constantly on TV and was written up in newspaper articles regularly because of her unique skills for solving crimes. The *Chicago Tribune* said that she's like a "real-life Sherlock Holmes."

As fate would have it—sometimes fate can be a wonderful thing—she was partnered with me. I was nervous as hell. Given her notoriety, I fully expected her to be an obnoxious overbearing bitch.

I was wrong. During our first day together as partners, I noticed that she was sweet and polite, as well as a hell of a good detective. She was also the most beautiful woman I had ever seen in my life. We were assigned to a case of mass murder in a mosque. As we worked the crime scene, I was blown away by her professionalism, not to mention her gorgeous face and cute little ass. As the days went by, I began to realize that I was not only comfortable with her, I was beginning to like her—a lot. Then, after a month of working together Bobbie said something I will never forget.

"I feel like I've known you for years," Bobbie said as she grabbed my hand, "even though it's only been a month. Remember, I've done a lot of research on you. And therefore, I've come to a conclusion."

"Want to share your conclusion with me, Detective?"

"I love you, Bob. I'm drop-dead crazy in love with you."

I felt like an emotional dam had burst. I told her how much I loved her, and shortly after that I proposed marriage, the smartest thing I ever did. I felt as if I entered a new world, a world that revolved around a beautiful woman named Bobbie Nelson. So now we're partners in every way. And we have a growing family, including Tilly, Jane, and Lucky, not to mention Steve, Jane's fiancé. And soon we'll have another baby. Bobbie is six weeks pregnant.

Bobbie and I are great at solving puzzles. The tougher the case, the more we like it. When Commissioner Ralph assigns us a difficult file, he'll often say, "This one's a bitch." Bobbie and I always look at each other say, "Yeah, but now it's *our* bitch."

But this bizarre Long Island quarantine has us totally baffled, nuts, stopped dead in our friggin tracks. We both agreed that we had never encountered anything so strange—or frightening. We tried to call my parents, both landline and cellphones. Nothing but the familiar sound of, "The number you are calling is not in service at this time." Same result with Bobbie's folks.

"Hey, Bob, working the phones doesn't seem to be getting us anywhere. Let's go into town and see what we hear."

We drove to Bostwick's Chowder House, one of our favorite lunch places. It's usually crowded with people, people who may have some ideas about this strange quarantine.

When we walked in the first thing we noticed was Franny Brighton, the Mayor of East Hampton, standing in front of the room. We'd become friends with Franny ever since we bought our house in East Hampton. She's short, a bit plump, but pretty nonetheless. She has a great sense of humor and is an articulate speaker.

"Hey, look who's here," she said when we walked in, "the famous BBs, the best detectives in the NYPD, maybe anywhere. Bob and Bobbie, I'm about to give these folks an update on this cluster fuck we find ourselves in. Please chime in with your thoughts." Franny, a Navy veteran, is well-known for her salty language. She once commanded a destroyer and was awarded 12 major decorations. She mustered out with the rank of captain after serving 22 years. Franny is a smart, tough lady. We found a couple of seats near the window. My head began to ache as I recalled that we were in this restaurant to find out about a quarantine of Long Island.

Franny grabbed a portable microphone. She wanted everybody to hear what she had to say.

"I think it's safe to say that this bizarre quarantine is the weirdest event any of us have ever encountered. I called the governor's office and my call actually got through. Sort of—I'll address that issue shortly. The governor often vacations out here and we've become friends, so he always answers my calls. We both commanded ships in the same strike force at the same time. I know his assistant quite well and also his chief of staff. None of them were there, including the governor. But the strange thing is this—I didn't recognize one of the three people I spoke to. None of them seemed to want to discuss the Long Island quarantine. Protocol requires that when a village mayor calls, she at least gets her questions answered. So much for protocol. The governor's office totally stonewalled me. Bob and Bobbie, anything you'd like to add?"

"Bobbie and I had similar experiences, Franny. We tried to contact the NYPD Police Commissioner, who always answers our calls. He wasn't there. We then tried the Chief of Detectives. Same result. Then we called the Director of the CIA, who is an old friend of ours. He wasn't there. And we noticed the same thing as you did, Franny—names we had never heard of before. Then we called the White House. We've become friends with First Lady Meg Fenton. She wasn't there, and, no surprise, we didn't recognize any of the people we spoke to. Bobbie and I have concluded that some person or some group is behind this crap. It couldn't have been coincidences that we spoke to a bunch of people we didn't know, even though we should have known them. Something big is going on and we're convinced it's criminal activity."

"When Detective Bob Lawton says something is criminal, I think we can take that to the bank," Mayor Franny said.

Frank Bracken, the East Hampton Police Chief, raised his hand. "Has anyone noticed that there is a new cast of characters in the newsrooms of all the TV networks. I've never seen any of them before. It's as if there's been a clean sweep."

Every one of the 30 some-odd people in the room nodded their heads in agreement. I noticed that most of their faces showed the same emotions I felt—fear and confusion.

"Bob and Bobbie," Chief Bracken said, "if you don't mind, I'd like to huddle with you after this meeting."

We both agreed.

"When I was a kid, my favorite TV show was *The Twilight Zone*,"

Mayor Franny continued. "It's as if we're cut off not just from the people we usually communicate with, but from fucking reality itself. You folks elected me to handle problems and to figure out what's going on. When I was a naval officer, I became accustomed to giving orders and expected them to be obeyed. But I don't know what orders to give or who to give them to. I have no idea what's going on, and from what I've heard here today, I don't think any of you folks do either. We may as well enjoy our lunch because we sure don't seem to have a handle on this. Obviously, this matter is my highest priority. Feel free to contact my office with any questions. And yes, you will recognize the person on the other end of the line. I think I'll have a martini with lunch."

After the meeting we walked with Chief Bracken to his office, which was down the block. Bracken babbled on nonstop, something he was well-known for. But something about the look on his face told us our meeting would be important—very important.

CHAPTER 3

Bobbie

Bob and I walked with Chief Bracken to the small East Hampton police headquarters building. As usual, he talked without letup. I think he was yacking to overcome his nervousness. He escorted us into his private office. Two cops sat outside the office. The East Hampton police force is small. Like any municipality, East Hampton has its share of crime, but East Hampton's share is sparse.

Holy shit, there was our old friend Mike Townsend, Suffolk County Police Commissioner. We knew Mike well, having had him and his wife Nancy to our place for dinner many times. Mike began his career as a uniformed cop and then rose through the ranks to become a detective, and eventually was appointed commissioner. He's a good guy and knows his stuff.

"I'm glad to see you two here. If you weren't, I was about to call you and ask you to come to my office in Yaphank."

Commissioner Mike Townsend is a giant of a man at 6'8," with shoulders like a linebacker. He looked scared, an odd look for a tough guy like him. He sat at a desk with his arms folded in front of him, wearing a look best described as a perma-frown.

"Is there a problem, Mike?" I asked. "We're surprised to see you here in East Hampton but not at the meeting with the mayor in the restaurant."

"Sorry for my cloak and dagger maneuvers, but in answer to your question, Bobbie, yes, there is a problem, a big one, besides the obvious problem with the quarantine. It's a problem for me but also for you two. Whoever is behind this goddam quarantine, and I have no idea who it is, has it in for senior law enforcement people. We have received information that whoever this is may be targeting me as well as the two best detectives on the street. I'm not telling you anything you don't already know, but you two are quite famous. That may have been good for getting you a big book deal, but it also puts a target on your backs. As commissioner of a large police department I'm keeping my service revolver on me at all times, and I recommend that you two do the same."

"Mike, do you have any idea of the whereabouts of Commissioner Norquist?" Bob asked. "We tried to contact him, as we always do, but were given the run around by some people we never heard of before. It's as if Norquist simply disappeared."

"I've been trying to contact Commissioner Norquist myself," Mike said. "He always answers my calls. Just like you, I had to wade my way through a lot of people I didn't know. I'm worried as hell that something may have happened to him. Whoever is pulling this crap off is acting a lot like the Mafia. Now I'm going to say something that may shock you. Although the county comptroller will throw a shit fit about this, I'm assigning two cops to serve as your bodyguards. I'm also assigning a slightly used car to you from our impound lot. I strongly suggest that you don't drive around in the car you arrived in. I know it's a rental, and somebody may recognize it. I also recommend that you wear disguises when you go out, maybe wigs and dark rimmed glasses. If somebody is out to get you, I suggest you don't make it easy for them. Your faces are well-known from your constant TV appearances. My daughter even has a photo of the handsome Detective Bob Lawton hanging in her room. Wear your guns at all times. This Long Island quarantine is the weirdest fucking case I've ever seen, and we need to adjust ourselves to our strange new reality."

I was shocked to hear Mike cuss, something he seldom does. It just reminded us how nervous he was. Like I wasn't? Bob and I have seen our share of being targeted, by the Mafia, terrorist groups, and others. We even spent some time as guests of the FBI in the Witness Protection Program. Looks like we're back to the same old stuff. When Bob and I bought our beautiful house with our book deal royalties, we expected our time in East Hampton to be nothing other than fun and relaxation.

After what Mike just told us, I didn't feel terribly relaxed. Nor are we having fun. And the worst of it is that we're stuck here, and we have no idea why.

"Bobbie and I are well aware of the need for security, Mike, especially after our Manhattan apartment was firebombed. We've tricked out our house and apartment with enough security devices to qualify them as safe houses," Bob said. "Are you sure we need bodyguards?"

"Yes, you need bodyguards. Now, I have a personal request. I want to deputize you both as Suffolk County PD detectives and I ask you to work with us. God knows we can use your brainpower. I'll never forget when you two gave us that seminar about computer sleuthing. I know you guys. You get antsy when you're not solving puzzles, and we sure as hell have one big puzzle to solve. So, what do you think? Want to join the Suffolk County Police Department?"

"Bob and I are NYPD, and I think it would be inappropriate for us to accept such a position without speaking to our commissioner, and we have no way to get in touch with him."

"I agree with Bobbie, Mike. I don't want to make a complicated situation more complicated than it already is. I'm honored by your offer, but we can't make a move without clearing it through Norquist. We think of him as a friend, not just a boss."

Mike looked at us with intensity written all over his face. He's good at that.

"I'm not talking about you resigning from the NYPD, just provisional roles as Suffolk PD detectives so you can have jurisdiction over cases you agree to take on. Bobbie, Bob, Suffolk County needs you, Long Island needs you. Hell, I think we'll soon find out that the whole country needs you. This mess is tailor-made for the BBs."

"I think we need a new tailor," Bobbie said, always the wiseass.

"Before you go, there's a guy here I think you should meet," Mike said. "I promised you I'd keep you up to date on anything strange, and what this guy has to say is definitely strange. Betty, please ask Lieutenant Gleason to come to this room."

A thin good-looking man wearing an Army officer's uniform walked in. Mike introduced us to Lt. Timothy Gleason. We both noticed that his uniform looked old, not that it was threadbare, but the style wasn't current, maybe of World War II vintage. It looked more like a costume for a movie than a military uniform.

"Lt. Gleason, please tell the detectives what you told me."

"What I'm about to say confuses me as much as it will confuse you," Lt. Gleason said, "so I'll just give you the facts as I know them. Eight hours ago, I was at my office at the Army Air Corps base in Montauk Point. I walked along a path that I had not been on before, when suddenly the ground shook and the daylight turned dark. After two minutes the daylight returned, and the ground stopped shaking. The scenery around me looked quite different from what it did before the event. The date was September 20, 1943. I kept walking and came upon a newspaper stand. I looked at a paper and the date read September 20, 2019."

Bobbie and I stared at each other, and Bobbie did an eye roll. Then we looked at Mike Townsend who closed his eyes and slightly shook his head.

"I was shocked as you may assume," Lt. Gleason continued. "I walked into a small building and asked the desk officer if I could use the telephone. The lady was polite and helpful and looked up a telephone number for me. I figured that under the circumstances I should speak to the police. She suggested that I call the nearest police headquarters, which happens to be here in East Hampton. I hitched a ride and here I am."

"Did you hear any stories similar to yours?" I asked, trying not to yawn.

"Yes, I'm not the first person to disappear from the base, but nobody knew what happened to them. I wish I could be more informative, but what I've just told you is all I know."

My thoughts wandered. Steve, Jane's fiancé, was preparing a birthday party for her, and we promised we'd be there by five. Bobbie and I exchanged a glance that said, "Let's get the hell out of here." We thanked him for his time and said we may have further questions. Further questions? I had no idea what to ask this character. Time travel?

"So, Bobbie, what do you think of our time traveling Army officer friend?" I said as we walked to our car.

"He's either full of shit or a lunatic."

"Yeah, but he seemed straight forward and articulate. He didn't seem mentally screwed up to me."

"Bob, you know as well as I do that psychopaths are talented at appearing normal. That lieutenant is batshit insane if you ask me. I mean, come on, time travel over 76 years? If you buy that, I've got a deal for you on the Brooklyn Bridge."

The next morning my curiosity got the best of me and I called Mike Townsend to debrief our conversation with Lt. Gleason the previous day and to ask about his current status.

"He's gone," Mike said. "Split, caput, out of here. He did leave a note for me saying that he thought he 'figured out a way to go home,' home being 1943 according to him. I think Bobbie may be right, that the man's insane, but he seemed like a regular guy. Like you two, I'm good at spotting lies, but I didn't detect any evasiveness from him. I think we'll need to scratch this off as one of life's mysteries."

We didn't know it at the time, but the mystery was far from over.

CHAPTER 4

Peter Solomon is chairman of an organization known as the Committee of Freedom, although few people ever heard that name. He's 45 years old, wears his brown hair in a buzz cut, and is medium height at 5'10." Some people find his steely blue eyes intimidating. He was meeting with his aide, Gloria Wetherill, at the Committee's headquarters in Provo, Utah. The building, which also houses Solomon's living quarters, overlooks Lake Utah.

Gloria wore a short tight black skirt that wrapped around her beautiful suntanned legs, and a blouse that showed considerable cleavage under her shoulder length blond hair. She knew she had a beautiful sexy body and didn't hesitate showing it off, especially to Chairman Peter Solomon. She made it her ongoing mission to get and keep the attention of the chairman.

"So, tell me about the Long Island Project, Gloria."

"Although it's only been 48 hours, Mr. Chairman, we must consider the operation a success."

Everyone addresses Peter Solomon as "Mr. Chairman," even his closest aides such as Gloria Wetherill. And she was a very close aide. Extremely close.

"Describe exactly what you mean by success, Gloria."

"All of the key players, from local governments up to the state and even the federal government have been reassigned, sir. Those who didn't accept reassignment are either in our custody or have been repurposed."

"And by repurposed, you mean?"

"They have been killed, sir."

"How is ingress and egress from Long Island being handled, Gloria?"

"We have a tank brigade consisting of 126 tanks patrolling the western shore of Long Island in Brooklyn and Queens. We also have an infantry brigade of 4,000 troops patrolling all coastal towns and cities. On your orders, sir, we have sealed off any tunnel or bridge access to the Island. We assigned a tank platoon of four tanks each to guard the following: the Queens Midtown Tunnel; the Verrazano Bridge; the Brooklyn Bridge; the Ed Koch (Queensboro) Bridge; the Robert F. Kennedy (Triboro) Bridge; the Throgs Neck Bridge; the Whitestone Bridge; the Manhattan Bridge; and the Williamsburg Bridge. Also, 25 of our larger gunboats patrol all the shores of the island. The Long Island region is, quite simply, walled off. Nobody can get in or out."

"Have there been any military threats against us, Gloria?"

"No, Mr. Chairman. Since you arranged for the reassignment of all military units, they now answer to a new leader and one leader only. That, of course, is you, sir."

"How is our Re-Education Program going, Gloria?"

"Brilliantly, sir, which is no surprise because it was your idea." Besides flaunting her gorgeous body at him, Gloria knows she can get his attention with flattery, and she does so often. "Hundreds are sent to the Re-Education seminars in Montauk Point every week."

"Is the press behaving cooperatively?"

"Yes, sir. The American press now consists of our people. The regular reporters will return to their posts after they've gone through re-education, but for now all new reporters are assigned by us."

"Would you like some iced tea, Gloria?"

Gloria stood and walked across the deck to get them a pitcher of iced tea. She was barefoot and her long, suntanned legs caught his eye as usual. She bent over as she poured his tea, being careful to give him a nice view of her ass.

"Thank you for your thorough and thoughtful report, Gloria. We will be meeting daily so you can give me continuous updates. Come to my living quarters this evening so we can fill in any details we may have missed. Good day."

Solomon enjoyed "filling in details" with Gloria after hours.

Peter Solomon prides himself on picking the right people as his aides, people who are a good fit. Ever since the first time he had sex with Gloria, he realized that she was a good fit, a very good fit indeed.

Peter Solomon walked to the edge of the huge deck overlooking Lake Utah. He lit a Camel cigarette and inhaled deeply. He strictly forbade any of his subordinates from smoking, but of course, different rules apply to the Chairman. "So," he said out loud, laughing and coughing slightly, "the Long Island Project is off to an excellent start."

CHAPTER 5

L oretta Brown and Randall Arkin are astronauts on the Space Station Liberty, owned and operated by the Committee of Freedom. The station is similar in size and design to the older Skylab, which was the first space station operated by the United States, managed by NASA. The Space Station Liberty's assignment is to observe the operations of the forces of the Committee of Freedom from the lofty platform of space. Their current task is to monitor the activities of the Long Island Project. Loretta Brown is the mission commander. She is also a senior executive of the Committee of Freedom. Brown and Arkin, both age 36, had served in the United States Air Force, having left the service with the rank of captain. After an extensive background investigation and dozens of interviews in Utah at the Committee headquarters, they were hired two years ago. Over 75 former astronauts had applied for the job, which pays $300,000 per year. Their current assignment is to track the activities of the Long Island Project, the most ambitious undertaking to date for the Committee of Freedom.

"It looks like the Long Island Project is going well, Randy," Loretta said as she looked at Long Island on her enhanced viewing screen. She wore a tight knit cap over her hair. She hated the way many woman astronauts look like the Bride of Frankenstein with their zero-gravity tresses sticking out in all directions.

"I get paid a hell of a lot of money just like you, Loretta, and I'm happy to keep my mouth shut as ordered. But I can't for the life of me figure out what this Long Island Project is all about. What's the purpose of quarantining Long Island?"

"It's really not complicated, Randy. Chairman Solomon wants our first project to be a large and defensible operation in a specific geographic area, one that is economically powerful. Long Island was a natural choice. Of course, it's strictly secret that the Committee of Freedom has anything to do with the Long Island Project. Our hand-picked agents answer all government phones."

"It almost seems like a huge conspiracy, Loretta. I've never seen so much secrecy."

"Yes, it is a conspiracy, Randy, a very powerful one."

"Why do you say that?"

"Because we control all the conspirators who communicate with the public, every one of them. Any time a phone is answered in any government office, you can be sure it's one of our people."

"What about the rumors I've heard about high government officials being kidnapped, including the Governor of New York State?"

"I guess we really shouldn't discuss these things, but it's only you and me, Randy, so I don't see the harm. Yes, the Governor of New York has been kidnapped, along with his entire staff. They are being held in a top-secret location. New York State is now under the control of the Committee for Freedom. Yes, the entire state, not just Long Island."

"What about the federal government, Loretta? Aren't they against us?"

29

"The federal government is completely infiltrated with our people. Some former officials have returned to their positions after completing the Re-Education Program in Montauk. That Re-Education Program amazes me. I've met a couple of people I knew before. After one week of re-education they seemed like different people."

"But President Harry Fenton is one tough character, Loretta. When he was in the Navy, his predecessor referred to him as America's greatest fighting admiral. I can't imagine him letting this out from under his control."

"This is Fenton's second term and he has only a year till he leaves office. His power at this point is quite limited. And we have a few of our people on his inner staff, unbeknown to him of course."

"I'm amazed that neither the Democrats nor Republicans have begun much of a campaign to succeed him. At this point I would expect to see huge political campaigns with constant advertising."

"That's because they're afraid to mount a campaign, Randy, scared shitless in fact."

"Why would they be afraid to put up a candidate?"

"That's because Committee of Freedom Chairman Peter Solomon plans to be the next President of the United States. Nobody dares oppose him. Nobody."

CHAPTER 6

obbie and I returned to our house at 5:15 after our meeting with Commissioner Townsend. No surprise, Jane was busy cooking dinner. I suppose we could do without Jane, but I have no idea how. We shared with Jane and Steve what we had learned in town. Little Lucky, our French Bulldog puppy, jumped against my knee and I picked him up. It somehow felt comforting to have a small friendly animal on my lap.

They both wore silly grins as we entered. I think Jane and Steve decided to *destress* in their room while Tilly was napping. We've noticed that our pretty babysitter and her handsome fiancé have a relationship best described as frisky. Jane and Steve told us they had been monitoring the TV all day, and just as everybody else in town said, there was nothing new about the quarantine. It's as if we've entered a new version of reality, a strange version of reality. We told them about our conversation with SCPD Commissioner Mike Townsend, and his warning that we may be under surveillance.

"We've been assigned two bodyguards and I'm ordering them to hang out here to watch out for you two and Tilly," I said as I cut into one of Jane's delicious chicken cutlets. "They'll be staying in the guest house. Put your car in the garage, and I'll rent a loaner for

31

you in case you need to run into town for something. Steve, I know that you have a concealed carry permit, and I suggest you keep your weapon on you at all times. I hope you won't need to use the skills you learned as an Army Ranger in Afghanistan. Please don't think I'm being too dramatic, but as of now we're all living in a different world."

"What are you and Bobbie going to do, if you don't mind my asking?" Jane said.

"Of course, I don't mind you asking Jane. As I've said countless times, we consider you and Steve a part of our family and it's our intention to keep you up to date on whatever we're doing and what we've found out. In answer to your question, Bobbie and I are putting our detective hats on, wigs actually, and are going to patrol around Long Island to see what we can learn. Stay tuned to the latest news from us, because you sure as hell won't get it from TV reporters."

"How is your latest book doing, Jane?" Bobbie asked, changing the subject. Jane is a skilled novelist and just had a book published by Penguin Random House. Bobbie and I introduced her to the editor-in-chief, with whom we had become friends after they published our book, *Detectiving*. Jane's novel, *A Gun Too Far,* is doing well. It's a police thriller, and Jane patterned the two main characters after Bobbie and me. She had the characters nailed so solidly, we thought we were reading about us. Jane loves to include her writing with taking care of Tilly, one of the reasons she enjoys her job as governess. She has tremendous powers of concentration and would write a few pages when Tilly is napping. Bobbie and I may have introduced her to the editor at Penguin Random House, but it was Jane's writing talent that got her book published.

"The new book I'm working on is moving along well," Jane said, "but I'm trying to include the Long Island quarantine in the plot."

"I only wish it was fiction," I said. "We're headed west where

32

we're going to try to figure this shit out."

At the word shit, little Lucky barked his head off and Jane gave him a treat.

Bobbie and I set out in our slightly used burgundy colored Lexus ES 350, courtesy of the Suffolk County Police Department. The car had only 10,000 miles on it and was tricked out with all the new automotive conveniences including keyless entry, GPS, and a backup video screen. First, we stopped at Party City in Bridgehampton to buy ourselves wigs. Bobbie, with her beautiful blond hair, is now a frizzy haired brunette. I bought a medium sized light brown wig. Our plan was to reconnoiter the shores of Long Island and report back to Mike Townsend. Mike insisted that we keep phone calls to a minimum for security reasons, and we agreed with him. Among the many things we don't know about our strange circumstances, we have no idea how secure our communications are. Our phones are secure and untappable, but with Long Island under quarantine, anything is possible. We would make one phone call to Mike to let him know when we were on our way back.

We made our way to Riverhead and the easternmost section of the Long Island Expressway. We were amazed at the lack of traffic. Well, maybe we shouldn't be surprised—there were few places to go. We decided to drive to the western part of Long Island, Brooklyn and Queens. Although the New York City boroughs of Brooklyn and Queens are geographically part of Long Island, politically Long Island consists of Nassau and Suffolk counties. Together, those two counties are known as Long Island. Non-Long Islanders sometimes find this shit confusing, but that's the way it is.

Bobbie and I both had recording devices to make notes of what we observed. We had cleaned off old photos from our phones to make room for the latest. We're preparing a large database on our computer at the house, including oral recordings. Nothing like a searchable database for yielding clues and information. We may be quarantined, but we're a couple of cops who know what we're doing.

The only news reports we heard that seemed to make sense were that all bridges from Long Island were closed to vehicular traffic. Make sense? What could possibly make sense to quarantine Long Island?

We drove into Whitestone, Queens, an area Bobbie was intimately familiar with, having grown up there. Although it's part of New York City, Whitestone has a suburban look to it with its single-family homes. We travelled down Clintonville Street toward Francis Lewis Park, named after Whitestone's most famous resident, Declaration of Independence signer Francis Lewis. It's a pretty waterside area nestled under the Whitestone Bridge. About one mile from the park, I pulled over and hit the brakes. In front of us we counted no fewer than 25 M1A2 Abrams main battle tanks. I recalled my service as a captain in the Marine Corps a few years ago when I commanded a rifle company in the city of Falluja in Iraq. I'm not unfamiliar with tanks and artillery—but this is Queens. And it looked like a war zone.

We lifted our binoculars and focused on the tanks, both of us making oral notes on our phones. We stared at each other for a minute as we finished our take-out coffee. Looking at Bobbie's beautiful face always calms me down, but this time it wasn't working its normal wonders. I felt nervous as hell. We put on our wigs, something we'd done many times before on various stake-out operations. The temperature was pleasant at 72 degrees, perfect for a walk.

"I don't see one American flag," Bobbie said, "nor do I see any insignia indicating that those tanks are from the United States Army. Bob, this looks like a goddam foreign invasion force."

We got out of the car and slowly walked toward the park. Commissioner Mike had the wherewithal to get phony IDs for us, which identified us as professors at Suffolk County Community College. He didn't think that our NYPD shields would be welcomed, and we agreed with him—especially when facing 25 battle tanks.

As a couple of detectives who have been on the street for a long time, we know instinctively how to look "nonchalant." We walked slowly, holding hands, telling each other jokes and laughing, trying to avoid looking like cops as much as possible.

I looked at my pregnant Bobbie, six weeks into her term, and asked, "Are you sure it's okay to walk, honey?" Her "baby bump" had yet to appear.

"Hey, Bob, do I need to remind you that I'm in great physical condition, just pregnant. Do you remember how many times we've made love in just the past few days? If my body can handle sex with you it can handle a walk."

A young corporal approached us wearing full battle gear and carrying a M16 rifle. We scoured his uniform and noticed no insignia that would identify him as an American soldier. His uniform looked Army, but nothing on it identified the man as American.

"Good morning," Bobbie said, with a big smile. Bobbie knows instinctively that one of her bright white smiles can melt the heart of many a man. Always works with me. Even with her frizzy dark wig, she looked gorgeous. I noticed the corporal giving Bobbie's beautiful figure a thorough going over with his leering eyes. The sight of his M16 dissuaded me from the thought of breaking his jaw.

"Halt, stand where you are," Mr. Foreign Invader said. "Show me your papers."

Show me your papers? His demand was the starkest example we'd seen of how much our world had changed in the past few days.

We showed him our Suffolk County Community College identifications.

"And where are you going?"

I almost expected him to end his question with the word "comrade," or "citizen."

"My husband and I are going for a walk through the park," Bobbie said in a non-committal voice. "Is that okay, corporal?"

Young Corporal Hard-on seemed taken with Bobbie's communicating with him.

"Okay, but no more than one hour, please. If you attempt to cross the bridge you will both be shot. And do not approach one of our vehicles (referring to the tanks) by closer than five feet."

So much for a walk in the park.

We continued on toward the bridge.

"Check out those other tanks, Bob."

Four more tanks were lined up near the water line with their big guns pointed toward the Whitestone Bridge. I felt like singing "America the Beautiful," but I didn't think it would be appreciated by our foreign invasion force. Who the hell are these people?

As we walked by a large boulder next to the river, we saw a young soldier enjoying a cigarette, obviously thinking he couldn't be seen. His stripes indicated that he was a private.

"Whoops, sorry," he said as he flicked his cigarette into the water. Bobbie and I have developed a sixth sense when we encounter a possible interrogee who may be cooperative.

"No problem, pal," I said, dropping into friendly-Bob mode. "I could use one myself but I'm trying to give them up," I politely lied.

"My name is Bob, and this is my wife, Bobbie. What's your name?"

"Jimmy Maxwell."

"Are you folks with the United States Army, Jimmy?" Bobbie asked as she offered him a stick of gum.

"No, we used to be with the U.S. Army, but we're now with the Committee of Freedom."

Bobbie and I looked at each other, our faces silently saying the words, "What the hell is the Committee of Freedom?"

"Of course, the Committee of Freedom," Bobbie said as if she knew exactly what he was talking about. Cool could be her middle name. "You folks have been busy, haven't you? Are you with a local chapter or headquarters?"

"We all work for headquarters in Provo, ma'am."

"Provo?"

"Yes, Provo, Utah."

"Oh, and what's that charming fellow's name, your leader?" Bobbie said, giving her command Masterpiece Theater performance.

"Peter Solomon, Chairman of the Committee of Freedom."

"Yes, of course, Peter Solomon," Bobbie said as if commenting on the temperature.

"Are you from Long Island, Jimmy?" I asked.

"Yes, I'm from Massapequa."

"I guess you're wondering what this Long Island quarantine is all about," Bobbie said nonchalantly.

"All I know is that it was ordered by Chairman Peter. It's known as the Long Island Project."

"Any idea when it will be over?" Bobbie asked.

"Well, it's not my job to ask questions, but Chairman Peter ordered the quarantine, so I follow orders just like everyone else. Most people I talk to don't think it will ever be over, that this is a new era for Long Island."

A permanent quarantine? Holy shit.

Bobbie and I looked at each other, indicating that it was time to move on.

"Well, it was a pleasure meeting you, Jimmy. Would you like some more gum?"

"No thank you. I think I'll climb onto the other side of the boulder and try to grab another smoke."

Bobbie and I walked back to our car, not discussing the conversation we just had with young Private Maxell. Detectives always avoid talking about a subject that may result in emotion, and it was difficult not to feel emotional after our talk with Jimmy Maxwell. *Never* show emotion if you're a detective. We cracked jokes and laughed. Just a couple of college teachers enjoying the scenery.

"Holy shit," Bobbie yelled as I started the car.

"Somehow I knew that would be your reaction. I completely agree. Holy shit. Our strange new world just got a lot stranger. After we grab a bite to eat, let's go to SCPD headquarters and huddle with Commissioner Mike."

I backed into a driveway and then turned left and headed back to the business area of Whitestone known among locals as "the Village." It was a pleasant area of retail shops in one and two-story buildings. I pulled up in front of a luncheonette where we'd get something to eat and maybe gather some more information.

Although it was noon, we were both surprised that there were very few patrons in the luncheonette. A Humvee with a 50-caliber machine gun mounted on its roof was parked in front. When we opened the door we heard a pleasant jingle from a bell mounted on top. An older man walked up to our table, greeted us pleasantly and asked for our order. The badge on his shirt indicated that his name was Harry. Bobbie mentioned that she grew up in Whitestone and they exchanged a few rounds of "you must know so and so."

I ordered a hamburger and Bobbie asked for a Caesar salad with chicken.

"I'm sorry, but we're out of beef and chicken. This goddam quarantine has limited our food offerings, to say the least. We only got one delivery in the past week and it was slim pickings. We can't get any supplies from anywhere off Long Island. Can I interest you in a grilled cheese sandwich with sliced tomatoes and a side of potato salad?"

We both said sure. What else was there to say?

"My wife and I went to the park under the bridge and noticed a large number of army tanks."

"And those tanks aren't just for show," Harry said. "I live down by the water and just the other day I saw a bunch of men trying to leave a dock on a large boat. A tank blew them out of the water without even giving a warning. This isn't the Whitestone where I grew up, nor the place where you grew up either, Bobbie. It's more like Berlin in the 1930s. The Committee of Freedom is taking over this country."

"What do you know about this Committee of Freedom, Harry?" I asked.

"I never heard about them before this quarantine. The outfit is run by a guy named Peter Solomon, and they operate out of Utah. They call themselves the Committee of Freedom, but they remind me of a bunch of goddam Nazis."

We finished our grilled cheese sandwiches and paid the bill.

The Committee of Freedom? Who knew?

And who knew what awaited us at Suffolk County PD headquarters.

CHAPTER 7

Bobbie

Detectives are trained to keep a calm demeanor about them, always a good way to stay focused on a task and to stay below prying radar. Just take a deep breath, slow down, and get the job done. But Bob and I were totally freaked out after our visit to Whitestone, my old hometown, now as familiar to me as the North Pole. It's a sickening experience to see your birthplace surrounded by battle tanks and heavily armed soldiers.

As directed, we pulled our Suffolk County Police Department loaner into the garage behind police headquarters in Yaphank. We had already called Commissioner Mike Townsend and alerted him that we were on our way. I looked into Bob's eyes, the most expressive eyes I could ever imagine. Just the right kind of glance from him and my stomach flutters. But the look on his eyes at that moment told me he wasn't feeling amorous. Besides being a wonderful husband and a sweet lover, Bob is one tough determined man.

As we walked into his office, Mike welcomed us and motioned us to two seats on the other side of a small conference table. It was only the three of us, I noticed.

"Hey Mike, you told us you planned on having the Nassau and Suffolk County executives as well as the Nassau County Police Commissioner in this meeting. But it's only you, me and Bob. What's up?"

"The Nassau and Suffolk County Executives have been kidnapped. The Nassau PD Commissioner has been assassinated. Our new world changes into another new world every few hours. The Nassau and Suffolk legislatures have unanimously elected me as acting County Executive for both counties. My new official title is Long Island Executive, although I'm still known as the Suffolk County Police Commissioner. I suppose I should feel like hot shit, but I don't. I guess you noticed that the hallway is full of uniformed cops outside my office. Everybody figures I'll be next—kidnapped or assassinated."

I had a hard time processing what I just heard. Two senior government officials kidnapped and a third one assassinated. Holy shit. This was beginning to look like war.

"I was about to say congratulations, Mike, but from the look on your face I don't think you feel like being congratulated. So, let me just say this. Bob and I are with you 100 percent. We have some interesting things to tell you about our day in Queens."

"Can you work from the top down?"

"Here's the top," I said. "Long Island, and probably soon the rest of the country, has been invaded and is under armed occupation. Bob and I went to the park under the Whitestone Bridge. We saw dozens of army tanks and hundreds of soldiers. Nowhere did we see an American flag or US Army insignia. The soldiers looked and sounded like Americans, but it's impossible to use that word to apply to them. Mike, we're under a military occupation."

"Who the hell are these people?"

"We found a talkative young private who filled us in on some of the details. He said the group in charge is known as the Committee of Freedom, and it's headed up by a man named Peter Solomon. Their headquarters is in Provo, Utah."

"But how does any of that explain what this crazy Long Island quarantine is all about?"

"It's known as the Long Island Project. Our talkative young private didn't seem to understand the big picture, but we know that there *is* a big picture. He did say that most people think that the Long Island quarantine is permanent. You heard me, fucking *permanent*. And it's not going to be very peaceful either. The waiter in a diner where we had lunch told us that he saw a tank open fire on a boat that was about to leave a dock, killing its occupants. And there was no warning. This shit is serious—and scary."

CHAPTER 8

October 28, 1943

Lieutenant Commander John Solomon, executive officer of the destroyer escort *USS Eldridge* (DE-173), called a meeting of the ship's engineering department. The ship was tied up alongside a pier at the Philadelphia Naval Shipyard. The war in the Pacific raged on that year, and the *Eldridge* was scheduled to steam to Pearl Harbor in one month. But LCDR Solomon had orders that had nothing to do with the ship's upcoming deployment to the Pacific.

A graduate of the United States Naval Academy, Solomon went on to get a master's degree in mathematics at MIT before he began active duty at sea. He was well known throughout senior naval leadership for his mathematical brilliance, although a lot of people were concerned about his secretiveness. Some believed he had his own agenda.

Solomon was tasked with heading up the Navy's most Top-Secret project, one that would become known as the Philadelphia Experiment. The experiment was based on an aspect of unified field theory, a term coined by Albert Einstein to describe a class of potential theories— mathematically and physically — the interrelated nature of the forces of electromagnetism and gravity. By uniting their respective forces into a single field some version of this field would enable using large electrical generators to bend light around an object via refraction. If that happened, according to the theory, the object would disappear from sight. It was Solomon's job to render the *Eldridge* completely invisible to the naked eye as well as to radar.

Three large electric generators were placed on the pier, 25 feet from the *Eldridge*. Solomon was not concerned about safety, because the experiment had worked on other objects, but nothing like the size of a destroyer escort. His only concern was that the experiment work. Whenever he was asked about the planned experiment, he changed the subject.

At precisely 10:15 a.m., Solomon gave the command, and switches were thrown on the three large generators. Dozens of eyes of those who had security clearance focused their binoculars on the *Eldridge*. One of the observing officers was from the experimental section of the Department of War, Commander Wallace Baxter. They expected to see the *Eldridge* become invisible for a few moments and then reappear. The length of the invisibility would be the next phase of the experiment.

What happened next was not what Commander Baxter or his fellow officers expected. Instead of becoming visible once again after less than a minute, the ship was "gone" for over 10 minutes. As soon as the *Eldridge* reappeared, Baxter's driver raced down the pier with Baxter in the sidecar seat of his motorcycle. He climbed the gangplank (which had not been raised before the experiment) with two aides. He was nervous because LCDR Solomon did not respond to his repeated radio calls. They saluted the colors on the stern and entered the quarterdeck where the officer of the deck stood watch. Had the OOD not been standing, Baxter would have confused him with a corpse.

"At the risk of asking an obvious question, Lieutenant, do you know why this ship was invisible for so long?"

"We spent 10 minutes in Norfolk, Virginia, Commander."

"But Norfolk is 200 miles from here."

"Sir, we appear to have travelled through space as well as time. Everything we looked at in Norfolk told us we were in the 19th century."

"Why is it so quiet, Lieutenant? I would expect to see the ship swarming with sailors."

"Follow me, sir. You may want to hold your breath first."

The OOD led Baxter and his aides down a passageway off the quarterdeck. The officer simply pointed before he broke down sobbing.

Baxter and his aides beheld a scene that would stay with them for the rest of their lives. One of the officers bent over and threw up on the deck. The bulkheads of the passageway were a spectacle of human bodies, fused into the steel of the bulkhead itself. They saw an arm here, a head there. The ship was quiet because most of the crew was dead.

The Philadelphia Experiment had not gone well.

CHAPTER 9

Bobbie

Bob and I had breakfast with Jane, Steve, and Tilly, cooked to perfection by Jane. This morning we were treated to crabmeat omelets and whole wheat toast. When we hired Jane as our babysitter, more of a governess actually, we had no idea that she loved to cook and was good at it. This was a pleasant surprise because the only thing I know how to cook is boiled water. We brought Jane and Steve up to date on everything we learned. They're trapped in this weird place just like we are, and no way would we keep anything from them. Tilly seemed a bit cranky, not that I blame her. Even Lucky appeared restless. They had never spent such a long time away from our Manhattan apartment.

We requested that they didn't walk outside the property with Tilly for security reasons. I noticed that Steve carried his gun in a shoulder holster under his vest. He'd been giving Jane shooting practice under the watchful eyes of our bodyguard cops. I had a hard time imagining sweet, gentle Jane packing a gun, much less firing it. Every day we gradually adjusted to our new reality.

Bob and I got into our assigned car and drove the 43 miles to SCPD headquarters in Yaphank for our next scheduled meeting. Not as close as three blocks to Police Plaza as is our Manhattan apartment, but not bad, given the light traffic.

We drove into the garage of the SCPD, as Commissioner Mike had requested, and then took the elevator to Mike's office on the third floor for our planned meeting. The place was surrounded by cops, which was no surprise, but I was shocked to see each of them carrying an assault rifle as well as a side arm. Are we really on Long Island? A man we had never met sat in front of Mike's desk.

"Bob and Bobbie, meet Dr. James Conklin, a history professor from Stony Brook University. He asks that we call him Jim. He has some interesting things to talk to us about."

Professor Jim was about 5'11," had light brown hair and wore an impeccably tailored suit. I figured he was around 50 years old.

"Pleasure to meet you folks. I keep up on current news, and I've seen you a lot on TV. I'm honored to have the famous BBs here on Long Island. God knows we need a couple of proven ass kickers on our side."

Not a stuffy professor, this guy. After a few minutes, Bob and I felt like we were old friends with him.

The intercom sounded.

"Mr. Langdon is here, Commissioner." Even though Mike is now the official, if interim, Long Island Executive, all his subordinates refer to him as commissioner.

"Drake Langdon is a guy I've been doing a lot of work with," Professor Jim said. "What he has to say has everything to do with my presence here. I'm writing a detailed history of the strange times we find ourselves in and I hope to turn it into a book. Any advice you folks want to give me on getting a book published, I'm all ears. I'm not sure if the book will have a happy ending. I'll let Mr. Langdon tell you all about himself."

Mike's assistant showed Langdon in. He was a medium-built man with the reddest face I had ever seen. Must be a bad case of the skin condition Rosacea, I guessed. He stood at the end of the conference table and smiled. Something about the guy told me he's accustomed to being listened to.

"Pardon my red face," Langdon said. "I've just spent a few days removing some heavy-duty makeup. If you saw me a week ago, you wouldn't recognize me. I'm an FBI agent, and I've just gone through the most intense undercover work of my career, under a different name, of course. For the past six months I've been working with an organization known as the Committee of Freedom, which I'm sure you've heard of by now. The Committee of Freedom is about as dedicated to freedom as a rattlesnake is dedicated to being cuddled. I'm not being dramatic when I say that this outfit is the most dangerous organization our country has ever faced—*ever*. Have you folks ever heard of the Philadelphia Experiment in 1943, or the Montauk Project from the early 1980s?"

I raised my hand.

"Detective Nelson?"

"Please call me Bobbie. In answer to your question, yes, I have heard about both the Philadelphia Experiment and the Montauk Project. I found the stories fascinating and read a book about each of them. The Philadelphia Experiment supposedly involved time travel. An American destroyer, the *USS Eldridge*, went missing for 10 minutes and was later reported to have travelled over 200 miles while it was missing and spent that time in the nineteenth century. Over 90 percent of the crew was killed, their bodies melded into the structure of the ship. The Montauk Project involved both time travel and mind control."

"And what can you tell us about those projects, Detective, I mean Bobbie?"

"They're conspiracy theories, hoaxes. In other words, bullshit," I said.

"Yes, at first glance they appear to be bullshit as you put it. But in my six months undercover with the Committee of Freedom, I've learned that they are extremely dangerous bullshit."

"I guess we're all wondering the same thing," Commissioner Mike said. "If you and Professor Jim are convinced that those stories are hoaxes, why are we even talking about them?"

"The theory that Jewish bankers controlled the world's economy was perhaps the biggest conspiracy theory in history," Langdon said.

"So why should we be concerned about that insane theory?" I asked.

"We should be concerned because Adolf Hitler believed it."

CHAPTER 10

Bobbie

B ob and I looked at each other when Drake Langdon said that thing about Hitler believing in the Jewish banker conspiracy theory. All we could see in each other's face was confusion. What the hell could Hitler's delusional thinking have to do with any of this? I figured it was time to ask for some clarification.

"Drake, I think I speak for most of us when I say that your Hitler comment doesn't seem to resonate. Would you care to elaborate?" "Yes, Hitler believed that the Jews were the world's evil, based on his insane belief in a twisted conspiracy theory. So even though he may have been delusional, his belief resulted in something the world will never forget—the Holocaust. Which brings me to another insane megalomaniac, Peter Solomon. I've studied this man closely for over six months. I'm convinced he's the most dangerous man in America, if not the world. A lot of our knowledge of him was shadowy—until I went under cover."

"Drake, do you believe he's behind this Long Island quarantine?" Commissioner Mike asked.

"He's not only behind it, he conceived it. With him, it's an intensely personal vendetta. He hates Long Island. How do you hate a piece of geography, you may ask? It goes back to the Philadelphia Experiment in 1943, before Solomon was born. A man who would be his great grandfather, Lieutenant Commander John Solomon, perished in that experiment, and Solomon's father never stopped talking about it. Peter Solomon grew up with stories about the tragic death of his great grandfather, John Solomon."

"But what does Philadelphia have to do with Long Island?" Bob asked.

"What began in Philadelphia found its way to Long Island, Montauk to be specific."

"What part of Montauk, Drake?" I asked.

"Camp Hero State Park, a 754-acre park which was formerly the Montauk Air Force Station. The camp is named after a man whose surname was Hero, Major General Andrew Hero, who was once commander of coastal artillery. A lot has been written about the place, including rumors that the place is used for experiments in mind control and time travel. Yes, you heard me—mind control and time travel."

"Yeah, but Bob and I agreed, as I believe the rest of you have, that those stories are just a bunch of idiotic conspiracy theories. I mean mind control and time travel? Gimme a break."

"Bobbie, remember our meeting with that Army lieutenant who believed he time traveled while in Montauk?" Bob said.

Mike Townsend nodded his head but carried an expression that said noncommittal.

"Bob, one lunatic doesn't prove anything," I said.

"Bobbie, you and Bob told us about your experience at the park in

Whitestone by the bridge," Drake said. "You noticed a lot of young men in military uniforms who spoke with American accents, but who seemed anything but American. Do you think a bunch of young guys would suddenly lapse into a different version of reality? From what I learned when I was under cover, a lot of mind control is going on, and it's happening in Montauk. They call it the Re-Education Project. How do you explain the strange characters you spoke to on the phone, characters who replaced the ones you should have known? And how do you explain the fact that every news reporter you see on TV you've never seen before. Where did they all come from? A different dimension, maybe a different time?"

My mind was aching from what Drake has been telling us. I'm a cop, a detective, trained in the law and law enforcement. Logic is my thing, but this guy was talking to us as if he was reading a novel out loud. I looked at Bob, and we had one of our wordless conversations. Our looks said the same thing: this is bullshit. But bullshit or not, Bob and I have some work to do.

"Bob and I are going to go to Camp Hero to do a little detective work. It's not far from our house in East Hampton. No amount of research can replace feet on the ground interrogating people."

"Bobbie, I urge you two not to do that," Drake said. "It could be extremely dangerous. If you ignore me, which you probably will, just make sure to obey the signs that say, 'Keep Out.' Yes, Camp Hero is still a state park and is accessible to the public, but there are some areas that are under strict control by the Committee of Freedom. Caution is the word of the day."

"Drake," Commissioner Mike said, "I'm not sure how much you know about Bob and Bobbie, but I'm here to tell you they're the best detectives you will ever meet. They know how to be careful. They also know how to uncover evidence. Don't worry about the BBs, they know their shit."

"They may know their shit," Drake said, "but the Committee of Freedom people do as well."

"Okay, this meeting is adjourned," Mike said. "Bob and Bobbie, report back with your findings. And be careful, please."

CHAPTER 11

Two hundred people walked slowly toward a large steel door on the outer fringe of Camp Hero, in the section occupied by the Committee of Freedom. While on the buses heading toward the camp, the passengers had all been mildly sedated. They felt relaxed and worry-free, even though they had no idea where they were going. They all had one thing in common—they were all former journalists and TV reporters. They were led down a long wide corridor by a dozen heavily armed soldiers. In smaller groups they entered elevators and began their descent below the earth.

When they disembarked the elevators six stories down, they were led down another long corridor to a large auditorium where they were seated. A few of them noticed large electronic devices hanging from the ceiling. The devices appeared to be some sort of weapon, each equipped with a long barrel that looked to be part of a gun. Still under sedation, none of them appeared to be concerned, except for one man, Ronald Porter, a famous and familiar evening anchor of *CBS News*.

"What the hell are you people doing with us?" Porter yelled, his sedative not working the way it was supposed to. "I gave nobody permission to take me here, and I don't believe any of my colleagues did either. I demand to consult with my attorney, *immediately*."

Many of the journalists fidgeted in their seats, nervous because of Porter's loud outburst.

A sergeant with an M16 slung over his shoulder approached Porter. He removed his rifle from his shoulder, pointing the barrel at Porter's chest.

"You have nothing to be concerned about, Mr. Porter," the sergeant said. "Please follow me and I will take you to a room where you can call your lawyer."

"I would like to join Mr. Porter," said Dwight Pinkerton, another well-known *CBS News* anchor.

"No more than you two," an officer named Victor Drummond shouted from the front of the room. He wore the bars of a colonel. He commanded the Committee of Freedom military unit at Camp Hero. "Our purpose here today is to give you folks an exciting and illuminating seminar. If you're in another room making phone calls you will miss it."

The sergeant led Porter and Pinkerton from the room, his rifle trained on them. Neither man was ever seen or heard from again.

"You folks have been hiking in the summer heat," Drummond said, "and I'm sure you can use some liquid intake. Enjoy."

A half dozen soldiers circulated through the crowd, dispensing 12-ounce bottles of clear liquid. The liquid was laced with additional sedatives.

The "seminar" began with a 20-minute video hosted by Committee of Freedom Chairman Peter Solomon.

"Welcome, my friends, to the Montauk Point location of the Committee of Freedom. You are about to embark on an exciting adventure, an adventure that will show you what our motto means. The motto is, 'the Committee of Freedom is the New World Order.' Soon you will rejoin your TV networks and continue your profession as working journalists. Ladies and gentlemen, welcome to the new world."

All of the group nodded and stared, the additional sedation having its desired effect.

Solomon showed various clips of Committee of Freedom activities, including its headquarters in Provo, Utah, shots of the Committee of Freedom section of Camp Hero, as well as a scene of the astronauts on Space Station Liberty.

When the video ended, the lights dimmed. Five large devices that looked like guns rotated across the crowd with the barrels pointed toward the audience. The devices scanned the crowd back and forth, as if making a video. A soft electronic hum accompanied the movement of the devices, along with occasional loud clicks. The sedatives were still in effect, but the mild intoxication was replaced by a coma-like stupor in each member of the audience. Besides the electronic hum and the clicking sounds, the audience was treated to constant messages, in a loud but gentle voice.

• "The Committee of Freedom is the New World Order."

• "Chairman Peter Solomon is your leader and savior."

• "Abandon your old ways of thinking; the Committee of Freedom is your new reality."

The "seminar" continued for another four hours. This was the first of five seminars that would be conducted over the remainder of the week.

Colonel Drummond walked among the audience after the seminar. He always considered himself as the first wave of quality control. He wanted to assess the thoughts of the audience after the first seminar. The Re-Education Project meant nothing if it didn't work as planned. He walked up to Walter Lipton, who, until recently was the famous and popular afternoon anchor for *ABC News*. His ratings were always close to the top of the charts. He was well-known for taking on the toughest of assignments and wasn't afraid to put his sometimes-controversial opinions on the line.

"So, Mr. Lipton," Colonel Drummond said, "I know that you are considered, if may use a cliché, a hard-hitting journalist. Do you have any thoughts on what stories you may want to report when you return to *ABC*?"

Lipton stared at Drummond, his face expressionless.

"I look forward to reporting whatever Chairman Solomon and the Committee of Freedom deem appropriate, sir."

Drummond smiled and patted him on the shoulder.

The Re-Education Project was achieving results.

CHAPTER 12

Bob

Bobbie and I drove from police headquarters in Yaphank to our house in East Hampton, a 43- mile trip. We planned to have lunch with Jane, Steve, and Tilly. We invited Jim Cronyn and Tony Lombardi, our Suffolk PD bodyguards, to eat with us. Bobbie and I are accustomed to being around cops, and we wanted to get to know them, the people assigned to protect us. We filled them in on what we learned about Peter Solomon, the Committee of Freedom, and Camp Hero in Montauk, which we would visit the next day. Jim and Tony are nice guys, and they loved our guesthouse in East Hampton. I think they enjoy the idea of being bodyguards at a waterfront mansion.

That afternoon, Bobbie and I decided to get some exercise in our pool, along with Jane and Steve, while Tilly was napping. Bobbie wore a bright orange bikini. It wasn't skimpy and could even be described as demure, but on her gorgeous body it didn't look legal. Pregnant for six weeks, she had yet to show the baby bump, and her amazing figure was on full display. I could feel myself stirring below the waist. Don't look at Bobbie, especially her body. Think baseball, yes, think baseball. Shit, this could be embarrassing.

Bobbie and I kept looking at each other, having one of our quiet communications. The way Bobbie looked at me I could tell that she was interested in a form of exercise other than swimming.

"Bobbie and I are going to catch a nap before dinner," I lied. A nap was the last thing either of us wanted. We walked up to our master suite.

"Hey, Bob," she said. "We've been neglecting something."

"What?" I asked.

"Us," she said, as she wrapped her arms around me and planted a hot, wet kiss on my lips. "We've been so friggin busy lately we haven't made love in a week. Let's get naked and climb into bed. I want to rock your world, baby."

She wants to rock my world? Wow, does she ever. Nothing rocks my world like my beautiful hot partner. I helped her out of her bikini as she slipped off my swim trunks. Now naked, we hugged and dove into one breathless kiss after another. Deep kisses, hungry kisses, demanding kisses. I stepped back slightly and stared at her stunning body as she stared at me.

"I notice that you're at strict attention, Captain. Let's put your lovely hard-on to good use."

We climbed into bed, and Bobbie rocked my world. And I rocked hers. "Take me to the mountain top, baby," she said, breathlessly. The mountaintop is our private code word for a mind-splitting orgasm. I took her to the mountain top and joined her there. Sure beats doing laps in the pool. I fell in love with Bobbie when she first walked into my office at the NYPD. I love her more every day, and it isn't just her gorgeous, sexy body, it's everything about her. I'm totally drop dead in love with her. She's all mine, and I'm hers.

After our "nap," we changed into jeans and sweatshirts and went down to the kitchen, where Jane was preparing supper and Steve was playing chess with Tilly. Yes, playing chess with our two-and-a-half-year-old. Jane had done an amazing job of teaching our Tilly to master a game as complex as chess. Lucky, the bulldog puppy, was sitting on Tilly's lap. From the knowing look on their smiling faces, I guessed Jane and Steve noticed our dumb grins. I don't think they bought our story about taking a nap.

"Steve had a wonderful surprise for me," Jane said, smiling ear to ear. "Since we have no idea how long we're going to be here, Steve and I want to get married as soon as possible. Steve called that nice guy, Father Rick Sampson, the pastor of the local Episcopal church that you take us to on Sundays. He's also pastor of St. Mark's in Manhattan. Fortunately, he was out here when the quarantine hit. Father Rick said he'd love to join us in marriage. He asked us when we'd like to have the ceremony and we both agreed that this Saturday, the day after tomorrow, seemed like a great idea. We already have our marriage licenses. Heck, we don't have a lot of planning to do, so we agreed we'd like to make it happen. Of course, it's up to you guys."

"Yesss!" Bobbie and I both yelled. We had planned on visiting Camp Hero in Montauk on Saturday, but we figured Monday would work fine. We've come to think of Jane and Steve as family, and anything we can do to help them officially become man and wife we will.

We moved out to the patio to have dinner.

"So, where do you want to spend your honeymoon?" I asked, realizing that it was a stupid question given the circumstances.

Steve and Jane looked over their shoulders at our house.

"We're thinking of a beautiful waterfront estate in East Hampton," Jane said, laughing.

"We should start to work on the guest list," Bobbie said, always the farsighted planner. Farsighted? We're talking two days from now.

We worked on the list with Jane and Steve. Because of the Long Island quarantine, we realized the list would be small. We invited SCPD Commissioner Mike Townsend and his wife Loretta, our two police bodyguards and their wives, Franny Brighton, Mayor of East Hampton, and her husband Bill, and Frank Bracken, Police Chief of East Hampton. Typical of a Bob and Bobbie event, the list included a lot of cops. We also invited our next-door neighbors, Jim and Grace Conklin, and their Golden Retriever, Maggie.

To no one's surprise, Steve asked me to be his best man and Jane asked Bobbie to be her maid of honor. Who would be the flower girl was a no-brainer. Little Tilly seemed to take her role to heart as she waddled down the aisle, accompanied by Lucky the bulldog.

It was great to see Jane and Steve say their vows and hug and kiss each other. I was happy as hell for them, great folks who Bobbie and I think of as family, our brother and sister.

Our little reception party was fabulous. Father Rick Sampson and his wife Janet played a violin and piano duet, *Summertime* by Gershwin. The prior owners of our house left a Steinway grand piano in the ballroom and Father Rick made it come alive. He and Janet played a few more Gershwin hits. If I closed my eyes, I'd think I was at Carnegie Hall. Lucky the puppy howled in harmony with the music, accompanied by Maggie the Golden Retriever. Bobbie and I danced a slow dance along with the newlyweds.

Pregnant Bobbie dutifully sipped her Perrier while the rest of us made good use of the booze and wine.

So, we find ourselves in a strange world, a bizarre world. Being surrounded by good friends makes it better.

Somewhat.

Monday, Bobbie and I would find out just how strange our new world is.

CHAPTER 13

Bobbie

Bob and I arrived at Camp Hero in Montauk at 9 a.m. on Monday morning, just as the camp opened to the public. We had just enjoyed breakfast with Jane and Steve, now Mr. and Mrs. Rankin, and Tilly. Even though they were technically on their honeymoon, Jane insisted on cooking and Steve helped her. We love those two.

Camp Hero is 14 miles from our house in East Hampton, so it only took us 20 minutes. That undercover FBI agent, Drake Langdon, seemed nervous as hell about our going to Camp Hero to snoop around. But Bob and I know what we're doing and being incognito is something we've done countless times as detectives. Just be cool, act nonchalant, and avoid acting like cops. A typical BBs assignment.

"Bob, I really think this is bullshit. They talk about mind control experiments and time travel. I mean, gimme a break."

"Bullshit?" Bob said. "Make sure you don't talk that way around Tilly."

"I mean, really, Bob. I think these conspiracy theories about mind control and time travel are total bullshit, sorry, I mean nonsense."

I looked at a map that the FBI guy had given us, showing where the crazy conspiracy theory says that the Committee of Freedom borders Camp Hero. I mean what should we expect, that some friggin monster is going to jump out of the woods? I would much rather be back at our house playing chess with Tilly. But as the great novelist Jack London once said, "You can't wait for inspiration. You have to go after it with a club." Same goes with clues. They don't jump up and bite you on the nose—you need to go after them. So that's what we planned to do that day, go after clues, even though I thought the whole idea was bullshit.

The first thing we noticed, because it stood out, was the huge radar tower that became operational in 1960 as part of the NORAD air defense system. The tower was 39 feet high and 126 feet long. It dominated the views at Camp Hero. I couldn't say the thing looked beautiful, but it was interesting.

We walked up to a clearing in the overgrowth. I looked at the GPS coordinates on the Waze app on my phone. It showed that we were in the perimeter of the area that supposedly is inhabited by that Committee of Freedom outfit.

"We should be careful, Bob. We're right near that Committee of Freedom area."

"Yeah, but that FBI guy told us to be careful to obey signs that said, 'Keep Out.' But there are no signs in sight. Let's walk a little further, Bobbie."

I couldn't disagree with him. Detectives have an organ in their body that generates curiosity. We walked through the opening in the shrubbery.

"Why would somebody create an opening in the overgrowth like this?" I said.

"I don't know, but let's be very careful, honey. I don't want you to need to run from something," Bob, my overprotective Daddy-to-Be said.

"Hey, I'm not even showing yet. I can outrun you, wiseguy."

"Let's keep our minds open, honey, as you often tell me. I've read a lot of reports that the whole idea of time travel is a possibility, certainly from a mathematical point of view." "Yeah, maybe I can travel back in time and undo my marriage to that wife-beating sack of shit I once wedded."

"Wow, you're testy this morning. How about a kiss?"

"Good idea. I love kissing you, baby. Why don't we crawl under a bush, make out, and forget all this bullshit?"

We walked about 25 feet further. Something didn't feel right. I had no idea what it could be, but I felt strange. It was the weirdest feeling I'd ever experienced.

"What the hell is that?" Bob said.

The ground began to rumble under our feet. Then it got dark, pitch dark—at just after nine in the morning. The ground continued to rumble. I looked at my illuminated watch, something I do instinctively when something strange happens. And something strange was definitely happening. Although it was just after nine, the sky was dark as coal.

After two minutes, the rumbling stopped and the bright daylight returned. It was 79 degrees when we began our trek, but suddenly it felt as chilly as October. I looked at the weather app on my phone to check the temperature, but the phone didn't work.

"Bob, check your phone. Mine's not working. It's like the battery suddenly went dead."

Bob checked his phone and it wasn't working either. The app icons weren't even there.

"Bob, everything looks different, totally different than it did a few minutes ago. A short time ago we were surrounded by tall trees, but now the overgrowth is gone and the trees look like they were recently planted. It's like somebody went through here with a gigantic weed whacker—a few minutes ago."

"Holy shit," Bob said. "Where the hell did that gigantic radar tower go? It just disappeared."

"It was right there two minutes ago," I said, pointing at the former location of the tower, my stomach doing triple flips. "And look at the size of those guns, Bob. They're gigantic."

"I recall reading that there were two 16-inch gun batteries here during the war."

"What war?"

"World War II."

We just stared at each other. We continued walking, our curiosity having taken charge. When detectives encounter something they don't understand, it's impossible not to investigate so we don't even try.

"Hey, Bob, what's that sound? Look up at the sky."

We could hardly see the sky because it had suddenly darkened with hundreds of propeller driven airplanes. The sound was like nothing we'd ever heard before, except in old movies. Bob and I are trained to estimate numbers by sight, whether it's people, boats, ships, or planes.

"I estimate there are 800 of them. What do you think, Bob?"

"I agree."

We raised our binoculars.

"Bobbie, those are Grumman Hellcats. They were built right here on Long Island at the Grumman plant in Bethpage. The Hellcats were manufactured from 1942 to 1944." One of Bob's hobbies is reading about military history. He could write a book on the subject, and I often suggest that he does.

"So, what the hell are hundreds of World War II aircraft doing flying over our heads in 2019?"

Bob didn't say anything. What could he say? There we were in 2019 and we just saw a bunch of military aircraft from the 1940s. We continued walking and came upon a one-story building with a parking lot next to it.

"Looks like they're planning an antique car show," Bob said. All of the 20 or so cars we saw were from the 1930s or 1940s. What the hell is going on?

"Maybe they're going to be in the same show as the vintage aircraft," I said, hoping my wisecrack would calm my fluttering stomach.

A man came toward us jogging. He slowed down and waved as he got near us, wearing a big smile.

"Hi. I don't recall seeing you folks around here before." He looked at us up and down, apparently startled by our clothing. We both wore cargo shorts and golf shirts with New York Mets insignia. He stopped to chat. He reached into his shirt pocket and came out with a pack of Lucky Strike cigarettes. He put one in his mouth, lit it and took a deep drag. Definitely not your typical jogger.

"These Lucky Strike people are terrific patriots. They supply free packs of Luckies to servicemen overseas."

"I guess they just want to keep our soldiers healthy," I said at my sarcastic best. I recalled that during World War II, cigarette companies gave away free packs of cigarettes to armed forces people, disguising the plan to get people hooked on nicotine as patriotism. But I didn't think the free cigarette promotions were done since World War II. I noticed a newspaper rolled up under his belt.

"Is that today's paper?" I said. Maybe a glance at the headlines will help clear my head with this strange shit. "Mind if I take a look?"

"Sure," he said, handing me the paper.

I glanced at the date on the paper—and my life changed. I showed it to Bob, and his changed too.

October 12, 1943.

He put out his hand. "My name is Dennis Remington, Army Air Corps Major Dennis Remington. I'm in charge of the military detachment here." We introduced ourselves, although I think we babbled, both of us still reeling from discovering that we had time travelled 76 years into the past. Could this possibly be happening to us?

"Are you folks currently in the military?"

"Bob was a captain in the Marines," I bragged. "He was awarded the Bronze Star for heroism."

"Wow, I'm honored to meet you. Was it in Europe or the Pacific?"

"I was in the Middle East, in Iraq. Hey, listen Major, I need to be blunt with you…"

"Please call me Dennis. So, what do you folks do?"

We weren't sure why, but Bob and I agreed that we would keep our college professor personas for the time being, and we shared our Suffolk County Community College alter egos with Major Dennis.

"Dennis, Bobbie and I came here about a half hour ago. The date was August 5, 2019, but the newspaper you just showed us says that it's October 12, 1943. Am I making any sense at all?"

Dennis shook his head and let out a laugh, as if he recalled being in this situation before.

"I'm off duty today. Why don't you two join me and my wife, Liz, for breakfast at my house. We need to talk. You're about to hear some amazing things."

"Hey, Bob, maybe that time traveling Army Lieutenant we met wasn't crazy after all."

"Or batshit insane as you also called him?"

"That too."

CHAPTER 14

Bob

As we walked to Major Dennis' house, Bobbie asked him why he didn't call his wife to let her know he'd be bringing guests.

"Call her?" He said. "How would I do that? We aren't near a phone." Holy shit, no cellphone. I guess we *are* in 1943.

The Remington house was a converted Quonset hut, a prefabricated structure of corrugated steel with a semi-circular cross section. It looked like a place where you'd store weapons and ammunition. I wouldn't expect to see the structure on the cover of *House Beautiful.* Inside, however, it was impeccably designed and furnished. Dennis introduced us to his wife, Lieutenant Liz Remington, the chief administrative officer for the base. Liz was a petite, charming brunette who moved like a bundle of raw energy. She didn't seem at all upset that Dennis surprised her with unannounced guests. I guess in a world without cellphone notifications, surprises are the rule of the day.

Dennis introduced us and then said, "Bob and Bobbie have come to us from 76 years in the future. Why don't you chat while I take a quick shower."

Liz seemed surprised by that news. Surprised, but not amazed, not flummoxed, not freaking out. Just somewhat surprised that we came from 76 years in the future, 2019 to be exact. I don't drink much, but I felt like I was smashed.

"Like Dennis, I'm off duty today so we have plenty of time to talk. I guess you have a lot of questions for us."

Dennis came back into the room after his shower, having changed into a fatigue uniform. Liz had just made a batch of scrambled eggs, which she served with ham, bacon, sausage, and home-fried potatoes. Bobbie had some eggs and a couple of potatoes but skipped the processed meats. From the living room we could hear a huge radio playing Glenn Miller music. I heard a big sound coming from the sky. I looked out the window and saw another huge flight of World War II Grumman Hellcats. It seemed like the perfect backdrop for *Chattanooga Choo Choo* playing from the living room.

"So, welcome to Camp Hero," Dennis said. "As you may have noticed, it's a strange place."

I looked at my watch, then at Bobbie. "Just over a half hour ago we were in the year 2019, so I guess your characterization of this place as strange is accurate."

"Apparently somebody removed the warning sign in front of the wormhole," Dennis said.

"Wormhole?"

"Yes, it's also known as a time portal. It isn't visible to the naked eye, but it's the strangest place you can ever imagine. We've lost quite a few people through that portal, and we've also had visitors from different eras in history drop by such as you folks."

"Hey, wait a minute," Bobbie said, "I just remembered something. I read a book called the *Montauk Project* and the author included interviews with dozens of people who said that they time traveled while in Montauk. I thought it was a lot of nonsensical stories made up to sell books, but after what Bob and I just went through, I think maybe the stories may be true. I can't believe I just said that. Also, we met recently—in 2019—with an undercover FBI agent who told us that this place has been used for two big and weird things: mind control and time travel. He also said that an organization is in charge of this. Do you know the name of the organization?"

We heard the Andrews Sisters singing *Boogie Woogie Bugle Boy from Company B* from the next room.

"Yes," Dennis said. "It's known as the Committee of Freedom. They're located here at Camp Hero, but not in the part controlled by the Army Air Corps. Army intelligence has been all over this outfit since they set up shop a few months ago, but nobody has been able to get a firm grip on who these people are. They're the most secretive group anybody has ever encountered. They seldom communicate with us on the base. Have you had any interactions with them?"

"Yes," I said. "In 2019 they quarantined Long Island, if you can believe that. Nobody is able to get on or off the island. They also seem to have discovered a way to control people's minds. We've encountered more incidents of bizarre behavior than we can ever imagine."

"Yes, we've heard about their mind control experiments." Liz said, "At least once a week we notice small groups of people being led through a large steel door which leads to an underground labyrinth. The underground tunnel system was designed years ago by the Army for weapons and ordnance storage but was abandoned."

"I think we should tell you about a man Bobbie and I met in 2019"—I can't believe I just said that. "He claimed to be an Army lieutenant from 1943, and he encountered a strange event that brought him to 2019."

"What was his name?" Dennis said.

"Lieutenant Timothy Gleason."

"Liz, give him a call," Dennis said.

"Hi, Tim, Liz Remington here. Please join us for breakfast at our house. There are a couple of people here who claim to know you."

Five minutes later in walked Lt. Tim Gleason, looking exactly as he did in 2019. I stood and shook his hand. He didn't shake Bobbie's, just took it in his and politely bowed his head. Men and women didn't shake hands in 1943. Also, in 1943 people didn't do bear hugs, although it seemed somehow appropriate.

"Tim is in charge of the military police force here,"

"Lieutenant Gleason…" Bobbie began to say.

"Please call me Tim, Detectives."

"Detectives?" Liz said.

"Yes, but we answer to Bob and Bobbie."

"Dennis, Liz, I must apologize for telling you that we're college professors. It's a guise that we use to keep under cover. We're detectives with the NYPD and we came to Camp Hero to investigate our strange circumstances. Having learned that we've time travelled 76 years, I think it's safe to say that our circumstances have gotten stranger. Tim, I also owe you an apology. After you told your story in front of Commissioner Townsend, I thought you were either a big liar or a psychopath. After what Bob and I went through, we now believe everything you said."

"Actually, Bobbie said she thought you were batshit insane."

He cracked up. "I've been accused of worse. As you 2019 folks would say, welcome to my world."

"So, Tim, you figured out a way to go back to where you came from?" Bobbie said.

"Yes, I figured that a way back could mean crossing over the place you went through. It's called a wormhole or time portal, the thing you encountered with the ground rumbling and the sky darkening. So that's all you need to do to go back to 2019. I have an appointment in 15 minutes, and I need to get going. I do hope I'll get to see you folks again."

"Before you make any moving plans Bobbie," Liz said, "there's someone who Dennis and I think you should see before you go back."

"Oh, right, Sergeant Murphy," Dennis said, "a weird case if there ever was one. You two have just learned all about time travel, and now it's time to talk about mind control. Sergeant William Murphy went missing one day. He was a damn good soldier and a fine MP. He showed up two weeks later having gone completely AWOL, a pretty serious crime, especially during wartime. He was brought to my office in handcuffs. I knew Murphy quite well, having served with him for over a year. But there was something about the guy that seemed off, way off. He was incoherent a good deal of the time, except when he was babbling about the Committee of Freedom being the New World Order. It's almost as if the guy's mind was stolen. He's still in the brig here, waiting to be transferred to a hospital in Washington for mental evaluation."

"Would it be possible for Bobbie and I to interrogate Sergeant Murphy?"

"I'll take you to the brig right now. It's a half mile from here. Do you mind if I sit in on the interrogation?"

"Of course, we don't mind," I said. "You're the boss."

"I think Liz should join us. As the admin officer on this base she knows Sergeant Murphy well. The two of us can help feed you information about him."

Dennis reached over and offered us cigarettes.

"Where we come from, Dennis, medical evidence is really solid that those things are bad for you."

He just smiled and lit up, giving one to Liz.

We climbed into Major Remington's Jeep and headed for the brig to interrogate the mysterious Sergeant Murphy. I was glad the Jeep was open because Dennis and Liz puffed away on their cigarettes.

The brig was small compared to others I've seen. It was housed in a one-story building surrounded by a fence topped with barbed wire. Two soldiers armed with rifles stood watch at the entrance. There were only 10 cells and nine of them were empty. The officer in charge led us down a hallway to the interrogation room occupied by Sergeant Murphy. Major Dennis had called in advance—from his landline phone of course—to let the duty officer know we were on our way.

Murphy, wearing an orange uniform, sat shackled to the table in front of him. He was ramrod straight and seemed to be looking into the distance, which was odd because he was only 15 feet from the wall.

"Sergeant Murphy, allow me to introduce you to two detectives from the New York Police Department, Detectives Bob Lawton and Bobbie Nelson. They have some questions for you."

As we discussed, Bobbie began the interrogation.

"Sergeant Murphy, are you familiar with an organization known as the Committee of Freedom?"

"The Committee of Freedom is the New World Order," Murphy said, staring at the ceiling.

"Can you explain what that means, the New World Order?"

Murphy took his eyes from the ceiling and looked directly at Bobbie.

"Abandon your old ways of thinking; the Committee of Freedom is your new reality."

"Have you had direct contact with any members of the Committee of Freedom?"

"I have met with Maxwell Solomon, Chairman of the Committee of Freedom, our leader and savior."

Bobbie and I looked at each other. In 2019 the chairman of the Committee of Freedom is named Solomon, *Peter* Solomon. Can it be that this committee is some kind of family business, passed down through generations?

"Have you been involved in any kind of educational programs with the Committee of Freedom?"

"Yes, it was my privilege to take the seminars from the Re-Education Project to rid my mind of stupid old ideas."

"Can you explain how the Re-Education seminars work? Hey Sergeant, look at me. Can you explain how the Re-Education seminars work?"

"It works the way our chairman designed it to work. He's our leader and savior."

"Why do you call this man your leader and savior?"

Because that's exactly what he is. He leads us and saves us. You too."

Bobbie and I spent an hour interrogating Sergeant Robot. I'd never met anyone like him. He didn't so much speak as let words come out of some memorized script. I also noticed that he seldom blinked. We got back in the Jeep with Major Dennis and Lieutenant Liz.

"I feel like I've spent an hour talking to a machine," I said. "You folks mentioned that you knew this guy for quite a while. What was he like before he went AWOL?"

"Believe it or not, he was a bright, funny, animated guy, nothing like the automaton you just questioned," Liz said. "If it weren't for his physical appearance, I'd honestly say that I never met this man before. Somebody or some people got ahold of this guy's brain and took it over."

"I hate to change the subject of this fascinating conversation," I said, "but Bobbie and I have a big concern. We have a little daughter back home and we want to see her. We've been gone for five hours, and our babysitter must be frantic. From what Lt. Gleason said, we just need to cross over that wormhole thing in the opposite direction."

"Do you remember where it was?"

Shit. Bobbie and I looked at each other, both of us realizing that we didn't make a careful note of where it happened, much less taking a photo of the spot, not that we could have taken a photo anyway with our cellphone cameras not working.

"I remember that that huge radar tower was directly in front of us, and there was a large tree to our right," Bobbie said.

"A large radar tower?" Dennis asked.

"Yeah, but it won't be erected until 1960. And the trees we see are nothing like the ones around us in 2019."

"When I met you folks while on my run, you were walking directly toward me. After you walked through the wormhole did you walk straight? I can drive you back to the spot I met you and you may be able to take it from there. I remember the spot, right next to a yellow fire hydrant."

"Yes, I recall us walking straight and we met you about a half hour after we went through that wormhole thing." I looked at Bobbie and she nodded vigorously. "Maybe if we backtrack, we'll get lucky."

Dennis drove us to the spot where we met him, next to a yellow fire hydrant.

"Hey, Dennis," Liz said, "let's be adventurous and drive Bob and Bobbie to where they think the wormhole is. Wouldn't you love to take a peek at 2019? If it works, we'll know that all we need to do is drive over the spot in the opposite direction to get us back here."

My God, these two are adventurous. Dennis drove at the speed of a walk after we checked our watches to mark off a half hour—*about* a half hour. My heart was in my mouth is a tired old cliché. But screw it, my heart *was* in my mouth.

We saw Lieutenant Gleason walking down the road to our right. Dennis slowed down to say hello to him.

"Hi, Tim," Dennis said. "Liz and I are tagging along with the detectives to the wormhole. We're heading for 2019."

"Mind if I hitch a ride?" Gleason said.

"Didn't you see enough of 2019 on your last trip?" Liz said.

"Just some unfinished business."

"Unfinished business?" I said. The guy was in 2019 for less than a day and he has unfinished business?

"Yes, I can't get that desk officer out of my mind, the one who set me up to meet with the police. I want to see her again. Call me a lonely widower, but I really want to see her."

"Hop in, you hopeless romantic," Dennis said.

"Bob, this is starting to look familiar," Bobbie said. "I remember that huge rhododendron off to our left, and that moss-covered boulder to our right." Thank God, Bobbie has a talent called eidetic imagery or photographic memory. She never forgets anything, especially if it's something visual.

"Look, there's that path we were on, the path between the shrubbery," Bobbie yelled.

"Please stop the car, Dennis, I want to get a photo of that path."

"Bob, remember, our phones don't work, including the photo app."

"You can take photographs with that little telephone thingy?" Liz said.

"Yeah, but it doesn't work in 1943."

"No problem," Liz said. "We have a camera in the Jeep. We definitely need a photo of that spot—assuming it *is* the spot." Liz snapped a few pictures and Dennis took his foot off the brake and the Jeep slowly moved forward at the speed of a walk.

We explained to them what happens while travelling through a wormhole, or at least what happened to us a few hours ago. Lt. Gleason chimed in with his recollections. I couldn't believe that we were explaining time travel to those two. A short time ago, Bobbie and I thought time travel was bullshit. Anything but.

The Jeep began to rumble and the daylight turned pitch black.

"Yesss," Bobbie and I shouted.

The rumbling stopped and the daylight returned.

"Welcome to 2019 folks."

"Please drop me off at the administration building," Lt. Gleason said. "That's where my unfinished business is located."

"Looking for a 2019 girlfriend?" Liz said, laughing.

"I guess time travel plays games with the heart," Gleason said.

We dropped Lt. Gleason off at the admin building where he could take care of his unfinished business and continued on to the spot where our car was parked.

I immediately called Jane's cellphone to let her know we were on our way.

"Jane, I'm sorry we've been out of touch so long. We'll tell you all about it when we get to the house."

"Out of touch so long?" Jane said, her voice sounding confused. "I just spoke to you five minutes ago."

Holy shit. We've been gone five hours, but Jane said we spoke only five minutes ago. Looks like we've got a lot to learn about time travel. Bobbie and I shot about 20 photos each of the wormhole location from various angles, so that Liz and Dennis could find their ways back. Dennis drove us to our car. He and Liz looked amazed when we pointed to the huge radar installation. It would be erected in 1960, 17 years from 1943. They were also amazed at our car, a 2019 BMW SUV.

Bobbie suggested that she ride in the Jeep with Dennis and Liz so she could act as an impromptu tour guide on our drive to East Hampton.

They were about to have their 1943 minds blown.

CHAPTER 15

Bobbie

Dennis pulled the Jeep in behind Bob and we all got out. Dennis and Liz stood silently looking at our house, shaking their heads.

"I guess they pay cops pretty well in 2019," Dennis said as he stared at our house. Bob and I would fill them in later about Bob's inheritance and our book royalties.

Maggie, the Golden Retriever from next door, came bounding over, her tail wagging furiously as she greeted her new friends. Our neighbor, Grace Conklin, accompanied Maggie. Having just climbed out of the pool, Grace was wearing a skimpy yellow bikini which looked great on her shapely body. I thought Dennis' eyes would pop out of his head, as Liz slapped his arm.

"Swimming attire has gone through some drastic changes over the decades," Dennis said, blinking his eyes.

Jane and Steve came to meet us, having just had a swim in our pool, Tilly in Steve's arms. Lucky and Maggie rolled on the lawn.

Jane was also wearing a bikini, which caused Dennis' head to snap in her direction. Liz gave him a frosty stare.

"Wow, check out this vintage Jeep. It looks like it's from the 1930s or 40s."

"It's a 1943 model," Dennis said, extending his hand, "the year we come from." It suddenly got quiet. Even Tilly stopped chattering.

"I'll prepare lunch," Jane said. "Something tells me you have a lot to tell us." She put on a robe over her bikini.

Liz seemed pleased that the subject of the conversation changed from Grace's and Jane's bikinis.

Yes, we did have a lot to tell them. Let's see, Bob and I time travelled 76 years into the past, interrogated a soldier who was brainwashed with bleach, spent five hours in 1943, although only five minutes went by in 2019. This will be an interesting lunch.

Bobbie and I then told Jane and Steve about our unintended adventure in 1943.

Jane and Steve are two of the most talkative people I've ever met. I didn't know if they weren't hungry or were unable to eat with their mouths open. They just sat there, seemingly dumbfounded by our story, and absorbed everything Bob and I had to say. They also looked stunned as Dennis and Liz described life in 1943.

Finally, Jane found her tongue.

"Do you think any of this has something to do with the crazy quarantine of Long Island?" Jane asked.

"We believe it does," I said. "Remember all the stuff we told you about the Committee of Freedom? Well, it was alive and well in 1943. Besides experimenting with time travel, that outfit has a program they call the Re-Education Project. Major Dennis allowed us to interrogate a soldier whose brain was so fried he couldn't discuss anything other than spout slogans he'd been taught. He was obviously brainwashed."

"Brainwashed?" Dennis said.

"It's a term that began in the 1950s during the war with Korea. Oh, I should mention that after World War II we were at war with Korea from 1950 to 1953, after which it split into North and South Korea. Technically, we're still at war with North Korea. The mind control program of the Committee of Freedom is apparently a highly sophisticated form of brainwashing."

"Speaking of brainwashing," Jane said, "the TV reporters we've been watching have been replaced by the old familiar faces. Their faces may look familiar but they're weird as hell."

She grabbed the remote and clicked on the TV.

"Good afternoon ladies and gentlemen, I'm Sam Petrelli for *News 12 Long Island.*"

I pressed hold and told Dennis and Liz that this reporter was one of the regulars who had been briefly replaced by people we'd never heard of. I hit play and Petrelli continued. They were amazed that I used a remote and could put the TV on hold. In 1943 they had a console TV with a rabbit ear antenna and a 12-inch black and white screen.

"And now for an update on the quarantine of Long Island," Petrelli said, "I interviewed Peter Solomon, chairman of the Committee of Freedom, at the committee headquarters in Provo, Utah. He assured me that he had no knowledge of the Long Island quarantine but seemed to think it is nothing to be concerned about. Here is a clip of my interview with Chairman Solomon:"

"The Committee of Freedom is keeping a close watch on this

situation," Solomon said, "Please keep your viewers updated and assure them that there is nothing to worry about. Thank you for giving me this airtime."

"There you have it, folks," Petrelli said, "words right from our leader and savior."

"Holy shit," I yelled, causing Lucky to bark. Jane gave him a treat. "Our leader and savior? Petrelli is the epitome of a hard-nosed journalist, but the man sounded like that robot soldier Bob and I interrogated in 1943. Do you think the Committee of Freedom may have put him through one of their Re-Education seminars?"

We decided to channel surf to see if we recognized any of the news anchors. Dennis and Liz were amazed at our TV remote control and the size and clear color image on the screen.

Station after station showed the familiar old anchors, but something was different. They all spoke like automatons and praised the hell out of the Committee of Freedom and that weird "leader and savior," Peter Solomon. It occurred to me that Bob and I didn't just travel through time—we traveled to a different reality.

Bob and I had a blast showing Dennis and Liz the wonders of 2019. They stood behind me as I typed into my laptop computer, a device that they found astonishing. I told them all about the Internet, email and texting, space travel, GPS, and nuclear energy. I Googled "moonwalk" and there was the famous photo of Neil Armstrong walking on the moon. I typed in "fighter jet," and on the screen appeared an F/A 18 Superhornet. Bob filled them in with as much as he knew about the difference between a Superhornet and the Grumman Hellcats that we saw in 1943. Dennis, a fighter pilot himself, was mesmerized.

"How does the war end?" Liz asked. "And when?"

We told them about the unconditional surrenders of Germany and

Japan and the atomic bombs dropped on Hiroshima and Nagasaki. "Germany and Japan are now our good friends and allies," I said, interjecting some good news into our history lesson. I couldn't help but feel that those two would find the year 1943 somewhat boring when they returned.

Jane took them on a tour of our kitchen. I would have done it myself, but I really didn't know how to operate most of the appliances. I heard Liz squeal when she looked at the dishwasher. They were both captivated by the microwave oven, as Jane demonstrated it by boiling a cup of water.

Major Dennis and Lieutenant Liz said they had to go back—back to 1943, as they both would be on duty the next day. They spoke nonstop about the experience they just went through. Our neighbor, Grace, walked over to say goodbye, her tiny bikini as skimpy as ever. Liz tugged on Dennis' arm. After saying their goodbyes, they boarded the Jeep and headed toward Montauk after I gave them a printout of the photos I took of the wormhole—the 2019 wormhole. I was about to ask them for their email addresses but bit my lip.

So, our little time travel adventure proved to be fun. But now we're back to the reality of the quarantine of Long Island.

Could it possibly be forever?

CHAPTER 16

Lieutenant Gleason walked up to the young lieutenant who helped him contact the police the last time he saw her. His heart fluttered as she looked up and smiled at him. When he first met her, he noticed a certain chemistry between them. And she's gorgeous, with medium length blond hair and the prettiest blue eyes he'd ever seen.

"I'm back, Lieutenant," he said, smiling.

"It's so nice to see you again, Lieutenant," she said softly. My God is this guy handsome, she thought. She looked at his left hand and noticed that he wasn't wearing a wedding ring.

"Please call me Tim. I didn't catch your name the last time we met."

"I'm Lieutenant Rebecca Jackson. Please call me Becca." She couldn't take her eyes off his adorable face.

"If you don't mind me saying, Tim, your uniform looks quite different from normal officer's uniforms. I noticed it the first time we met, but you seemed to be in a hurry and I didn't want to slow you down."

"That's because I came here from 1943."

She cracked up laughing.

"I've heard some interesting pickup lines over the years, but that one takes the prize."

"I have some interesting stories I'd like to share with you, Becca. May I take you to lunch?"

"I've never been asked on a date by a guy from 1943, so I don't see how I can turn you down." This guy's got a strange sense of humor, she thought, but he's so friggin good looking she didn't want to resist his lunch invitation.

"A date?" he said. "I like the sound of that."

"I get off duty in 15 minutes. Can you stick around?" (*so I can stare at your handsome puss.*)

"I'd be happy to, Becca. You pick the restaurant. I'll ask you to drive because I don't have a car. I left it in 1943."

"Sure thing, Tim" she said, laughing. This man is the cutest nut she'd ever met.

———————

They drove to Gosman's Dock, a pretty waterfront restaurant with a beautiful view of Montauk Harbor. She chose it because the atmosphere is somewhat romantic. *What the hell am I doing, she thought. This isn't like me. I think of myself as a by-the-books Army officer, not some flirtatious floozie. But there's something about this guy that I find extremely attractive. Besides his Hollywood good looks, he has a sweet, gentle way about him. And he has a great sense of humor with his time travel stories.*

"I have a gift certificate for this place that I got for my birthday,

Tim, so I insist that this be my treat."

"Hey, Becca, that won't be necessary." He then glanced at the prices on the menu, 2019 prices, not 1943. He expected to see prices at or below one dollar, but he was shocked to see the average entry was over $20. "But on second thought I accept your generous offer."

"So, what's with these time travel jokes you've been telling me?"

"You're not the kind of woman I would joke with. I must admit something that I'm going to embarrass myself with, Becca, but I find you extremely attractive. I hope I'm not being overly forward, but I have to admit the truth. I find myself drawn to you."

"Well, now I'm going to embarrass myself. I find you very attractive, and I admit that I find myself drawn to you too. I felt it the first time we met, and I confess that I've thought about you constantly since then. I find you a very comfortable man to be with, but I'm not used to flirting—which is what we're doing. But to get back to my question about your time travel jokes…"

"Did you ever hear about the Montauk Project?"

"Yes, I have, and I always thought it was a bunch of nonsense."

"Well it isn't nonsense, Becca, it's the truth. I learned on my last trip to this year, that time travel and Camp Hero are two ideas that belong together. Are you familiar with the area of Camp Hero that's dotted with signs warning people to keep out?"

"Yes, I am familiar with those signs, but nobody has given me an explanation. So, what are the warnings all about? Is there some kind of danger?"

"The signs are in front of a wormhole, also known as a time portal. Cross that portal and you find yourself in 1943. No, I'm not joking, it's the truth. I would never tell you anything but the truth. I came here from the year 1943."

"My God, that would make you over 100 years old."

"I keep myself in pretty good shape, wouldn't you agree?"

"Yes, I definitely agree. You're in fabulous shape. I have a confession."

"What's that?"

"I have a hard time keeping my eyes off you, Tim. I think I like you—a lot."

"Well, I need to make a confession too, Becca. I'm crazy about you. Are you seeing anyone? I'm sure a beautiful woman like you must have a pack of guys in pursuit."

"No, I'm not attached. Tim, I find this lunch unbelievable. I'm not the flirting type, but there's something about you that causes my mouth to fly in its own direction. I'm happy that you stopped to ask for directions a while ago. And I'm definitely happy that you came back. Good grief, we're talking like a couple of long-time boy and girlfriends."

"Do you believe in fate, Becca?"

"I do," she said, staring into his eyes. "I think fate brought us together. I think it's our destiny to be boy and girlfriend. And maybe more. There's something about you, Tim."

"Correction. There's something about *us*."

CHAPTER 17

Two Months Later

I just married the most wonderful woman I've ever met. Becca Jackson wrapped herself around my heart in a way I could only imagine. I feel like I'm dreaming. Here I am in 2019, having time travelled from 1943, and I'm so happy I feel like I could explode with joy. Besides her gorgeous looks, Becca has a sweet way about her that simply melts my heart.

Becca and I have become good friends with a couple of great people, Detectives Bob Lawton and Bobbie Nelson. When I first met them in police headquarters in East Hampton, they thought I was nuts with my talk about time travel. Then they traveled through time when they visited Montauk, and they no longer see me as a "batshit insane," as Bobbie put it. Bob agreed to be my best man and Bobbie served as Becca's maid of honor. They even threw our wedding reception at their beautiful home in East Hampton. Bob and Bobbie have a lot of influence, I soon learned. They convinced Commissioner Townsend to give me a job as a detective with the Suffolk County Police Department. My experience as a military cop sold him on the idea. I was happy to land that job because the few

1943 dollars I had in my pocket would not go very far in 2019. Maybe I'll be able to get one of those credit card things they seem so fond of in this year. My job now is to help the BBs do whatever we can to end the quarantine of Long Island.

Becca, who inherited a small fortune from her late banker father, owns a lovely house in Bridgehampton. She insisted on putting me on the deed. Becca still works as an Army officer at Camp Hero in Montauk. Every time I look at her beautiful face, I consider myself one lucky man. I like it here in 2019—with my beautiful new wife.

CHAPTER 18

Two hundred mid-level officials from the federal government got off their buses and walked toward the huge steel doorway that led to the Re-Education Project auditorium. As always, they were heavily sedated. They all worked for the United States Department of State. The group had all gathered in a large hotel auditorium in Washington the previous day, having been fed a made-up story that the conference concerned new statutory changes to State Department policy. Major Aldo Rizzuto was the officer in charge of this week's Re-Education Project for the Committee of Freedom. Deputy Undersecretary of State James Franklin had convened the meeting. Franklin, who had been with the State Department for 18 years, had gone through the Re-Education Project seminars a month before. He was now a high-level insider for the Committee of Freedom, although his title had not been made official. Franklin sat in one of the buses that would take the group from Washington, D.C. to Montauk Point, Long Island. Although Major Rizzuto was the officer in charge of the seminars, Franklin was the chief advisor, and wielded considerable power. Even long-time members of the Committee of Freedom recognized that Franklin was a man to be reckoned with.

When they arrived in Montauk, they disembarked the buses and the group was led to the Re-Education Project building. They took the elevators that led to the underground auditorium, none of them suspecting anything out of the ordinary. The sedatives had done their work. As they took their seats in the auditorium, the gentle Bach Partita Number 2 in D minor played over the speakers.

The weeklong seminars of the Re-Education Project always began with a 20-minute video introduction narrated by the Committee of Freedom Chairman Peter Solomon. But this series of seminars began with a personal appearance and speech by Solomon himself. His Committee of Freedom plane went through the Long Island quarantine without a problem. As the music ended, Solomon sat on the dais along with Major Rizzuto and Deputy Undersecretary Franklin.

"Ladies and gentlemen," Major Rizzuto said, "we have the special honor to have with us our leader and savior, Chairman Peter Solomon. Please give him a warm round of applause."

Leader and savior? a few in the crowd thought, despite their sedatives. What the hell is that all about?

"My friends," Solomon began, "you are in for a special treat in this series of seminars. You are all highly placed officials with the United States Department of State, and you will soon return to your duties in Washington, armed with some new talents and ideas you will learn in the seminars. Welcome to the New World Order. You will soon learn that the old ways of doing things, including running government agencies, will change for the better. You will abandon the old ways of thinking and acting and will help lead the government into exciting new directions. Welcome to the New Reality, the New Reality of the Committee of Freedom, the New World Order."

When Solomon finished his comments, five large electronic units began to slowly make their way along tracks in the ceiling. Attached to the devices were objects that looked like gun barrels. As the devices made their way back and forth on tracks in the ceiling, the barrel-like appendages pointed randomly to members of the audience. The electronic hum of the devices was punctuated by loud clicking noises.

After two hours, Deputy Undersecretary Fleming made his way among the audience, randomly chatting with a few of his colleagues. He approached Hiram Smith, Assistant Secretary of State for the Middle East, and asked him what he intended to do upon his return to Washington. Hiram Smith was well known for his hard-nosed approach to his job. He gave no bullshit, nor did he accept any.

"I intend to do whatever Chairman Solomon determines is best for the country," Smith said. "He is our leader and savior and whatever he thinks best is exactly what I will pursue."

Fleming smiled and patted him on the shoulder.

CHAPTER 19

G ood evening ladies and gentlemen and welcome to *Special Report*. I'm your *Fox News* anchor, Bret Baier. Tonight, we are looking at political history, the soon-to-come first ever nominating convention of the mysterious organization, the Committee of Freedom, which is now a political party. The Committee of Freedom has been described by some as a shadowy organization, cloaked in secrecy. The man who heads the committee is Peter Solomon, who conducts his affairs from the headquarters of the party in Provo, Utah. There have been countless reports that the infamous quarantine of Long Island is the brainchild of the Committee of Freedom, although Solomon and his people vigorously deny it. We have been told by inside sources that the quarantine is part of something known as the Long Island Project, and the quarantine is but one small part of the project.

"I'm not speculating when I say that the hands-down favorite of the organization to be nominated to run for President of the United States is none other than Chairman Peter Solomon himself. President Harry Fenton is serving his last few months in office and will step down this coming January.

"President Fenton hasn't been shy about criticizing the Committee of Freedom and its chairman. I'm pleased to say that we have with us on the line President Fenton himself, who will share his thoughts with us."

The president sat in the oval office, the seal of the presidency behind his shoulders.

"Good evening Mr. President and thank you for joining us on *Special Report.* Please give us your thoughts on this new political party, the Committee of Freedom."

"Thank you for having me, Bret. Yes, I'm extremely concerned about this new party, the Committee of Freedom, one that none of us ever heard of a short time ago. Our democracy thrives on transparency and openness, and despite its name, the Committee of Freedom seems to be about anything but freedom. Although they vigorously deny it, it appears that the Committee of Freedom is the operating force behind the bizarre quarantine of Long Island."

"Mr. President, if I may, most commentators consider the quarantine to be patently illegal. Is there anything the federal government can do to put an end to it?"

"As you know, Bret, I've ordered the Justice Department to intervene, but they have come up against a huge problem. Many government officials, both local and state, are voluntarily complying with the quarantine. Our officials have found that even some members of my administration are in compliance. The Justice Department is vigorously looking into that issue. Although it isn't often that a sitting president throws himself into the political arena when he's serving the last few months of his term, I urge the American people to be extremely cautious with the Committee of Freedom. The organization is an anathema to our American way of doing things. Their motto, 'A New World Order,' should strike fear into the hearts of freedom-loving Americans. Thank you for inviting me on, Bret. If you have any other questions for the White

House, just give us a call."

"Thank you. Mr. President.

"So, there you have it, folks, words of warning from none other than the President of the United States. We will be bringing you up to date on this amazing development."

CHAPTER 20

Grant Cummings, the General Manager of the Venetian Hotel in Las Vegas, decided to take a drastic step with his hotel's way of operating. While at a trade show in Texas, he was amazed at how robotics has transformed the way business is conducted, especially at hotels. He decided, on the second day of the show, that the Venetian would become radically automated, more so than any other hotel. At over 7,000 rooms, the Venetian is the largest hotel in Las Vegas and one of the largest in the world. After clearing the idea with his board of directors, he met with a representative of Robot Depot, the automation giant, and planned out his strategy. Each floor would be equipped with robotic vacuum cleaners, as well as automated bathroom cleaning devices. The huge windows of the Venetian would be cleaned with robots. Additional robots would be used to clean the reception area and all conference rooms. Cummings grew up in a working-class family, and part of him hated the idea of displacing workers with machines, but he felt that he couldn't ignore the changing reality of automation and the vast amount of money that could be saved. His calculations showed him that the Venetian could save $1 million a year on salaries by automating the hotel. He placed an initial order for 2,500 robots from the Robot Depot plant in Los Angeles. He couldn't order them from headquarters because it was on quarantined Long Island.

———————

Two Weeks Later

Grant Cummings couldn't remember when he had a worse day. The 2,500 robots he ordered from Robot Depot had just been activated. Within the first 10 minutes there were five incidents of robotic floor cleaners crashing at high speed into hotel guests, resulting in several leg and ankle fractures. Then it appeared that the filters and dirt capturing compartments on the vacuums stopped working. The machines simply took in the dirt and spit it out the back, creating an environment of swirling dust and dirt on all floors and in every room. One of the window washing robots exploded, knocking out a huge window, sending it crashing to the sidewalk hundreds of feet below. Dozens of pedestrians were injured, one critically.

Recognizing that it had a huge public relations problem, Robot Depot management offered to dispatch key executives from the quality control department, but, because the company was located on Long Island, nobody could fly to Las Vegas because of the Long Island quarantine. They sent a group from one of its satellite locations, but they were not the skilled engineers from the home office.

Cummings ordered all the robots deactivated. Because the automation program had resulted in large layoffs, there weren't enough cleaning people to handle the guests' rooms. Cummings wondered if he could get a job dealing cards in the casino.

CHAPTER 21

Bobbie

The land line phone rang. Like many people, Bob and I have a land line phone, although we spent most of our telephone time on our cellphones. Jane picked it up

"It's a lady named Jenny Bateman for you or Bob, Bobbie."

Jenny Bateman, CEO of Robot Depot from Hauppauge, Long Island, had become good friends with Bob and me. She was critical in bringing an end to the use of her company's flying drones as instruments of terror used to attack athletic stadiums, which had resulted in thousands of deaths and countless injuries. A terrorist group had set its sights on attacking football stadiums while games were being played. That was one weird case, but Jenny's sharp thinking and quick actions brought an end to the terrorism. She also wrote a terrific book which I loved, titled, appropriately enough, *Robot Depot*. She had given us a signed copy.

Jenny Bateman is the real deal. A decisive business executive, she continuously sends her company's stock price into orbit. She's also an unabashed patriot, and won't stand for anybody messing with her country's affairs.

"Jenny, good to hear your voice, my friend," I said. "I'm putting you on speaker so Bob can join in. What's up?"

"Thank God you two are on Long Island, Bobbie. I have a situation you may find interesting. I've heard sporadic reports about people acting strangely since this fucking quarantine started."

Jenny is well-known for her blunt language.

"Those reports are becoming less sporadic, Jenny, and more like every day."

"Some of my executives at Robot Depot have been acting more than strange recently. It happened after each of them took a one-week vacation. When they left, they looked and sounded normal, but when they returned, we noticed that they started to act weird. They speak in monotones and spout crap about something called 'the New World Order.' You can have a livelier conversation with some of my robots than with these overpaid clowns. Yesterday afternoon, the shit hit the fan. We had just filled a large order for floor and window-cleaning robots from none other than the huge Venetian Hotel in Las Vegas. To cut right to the chase, our execs from quality control apparently fell asleep at the switch. The fucking robots started acting like terrorists, mowing down guests. They charged at guests at high speed, breaking ankles and legs. The filters on the vacuums stopped working which resulted in flying dirt all over the hotel. One of the window-cleaning bots exploded, knocking out a huge window and sending it to the ground, seriously injuring dozens of pedestrians, one critically. We're going to get our asses sued, I'm sure. But, hey, these are my problems, not the NYPD's. The reason I called you guys is that you tend to be on top of things, and I was wondering if you heard about people acting strangely."

"I think Bobbie and I should meet you at Robot Depot," Bob said. "I'd love to interrogate some of those strange-acting managers. How about tomorrow morning at nine?"

"Great. Breakfast is on me," Jenny said. "It will be a pleasure meeting with old friends and take a break from talking to lawyers all the time. See you tomorrow, BBs."

"Did you catch what she said, Bob. Some of her managers talk about 'the New World Order.' Sound familiar?"

"Yes, it sounds damn familiar. This crap is starting to look like a bigger problem than I first thought. And I noticed that she said the weird managers are from quality control. What better department to have a brainwashed nut job cause problems?"

CHAPTER 22

Bob

Bobbie and I pulled up to Robot Depot headquarters in Hauppauge for our working breakfast with Jenny Bateman. The Robot Depot "campus" is a 30-acre plot surrounded by beautiful trees and shrubbery. The grounds are kept attractive by a small army of robotic gardening devices. The company uses the grounds as a test facility for its landscaping division. As we walked through the front door we were greeted by a pretty woman in a bright yellow dress. As she welcomed us, we noticed that her voice sounded strange. We suddenly realized that she was a robot.

The pretty robot led us into the executive dining room, where Jenny stood waiting for us. The room was large and tastefully decorated. Little robots on wheels quietly circulated with pots of coffee and snacks. The executive dining room is down the hall from the employee dining room, where all the meals are free. Jenny takes good care of her people. A waitress—a real human being—came over to take our orders. My pregnant Bobbie judiciously ordered items high in protein.

Besides being the CEO of a giant corporation, Jenny Bateman is a strikingly beautiful woman, probably the sexiest CEO in American business. She's a tall at 5'11" and wears her lovely soft brown hair in wavy curls that touch her shoulders. Her long suntanned legs were on prominent display below her medium length dress. If legs could kill, Jenny should be arrested.

As Jenny munched on a bagel, she quietly brought our attention to a few of the strange acting executives who were in the dining room, without pointing her finger of course. Jenny's a class act.

"That tall guy with gray hair seated next to the window is one of the stranger ones. He never shuts up about the 'New World Order,' and a man he calls our 'leader and savior,' some guy named Peter Solomon. I caught President Fenton being interviewed on *Fox* last night. He seemed pretty upset about that man, who apparently is the chairman of an outfit called the Committee of Freedom. Could there possibly be a connection to the strange behavior in people?"

Bobbie and I told Jenny about our experience in Montauk, leaving out the time-travel details. We'd tell her about that later, but for now we want to focus on our task at hand—mind control.

"Here's some really creepy information, Jenny. That Committee of Freedom outfit runs a series of seminars called the Re-Education Project. From what we've learned so far, its purpose is to brainwash people and take over their minds. When we interrogate your guys, we're going to ask them if they'd been to Montauk recently. My gut tells me that your people may have been 're-educated.' When you told us that some of them spout the phrase 'New World Order,' it makes me almost certain that they've gone through the program."

"We're ahead of you on that one, Bob and Bobbie. All our executives are required to have the tracking module on their phones active at all times so we can get in touch with them. The GPS coordinates on each of their phones showed that they were, indeed, in Montauk before they returned here."

Jenny's assistant led us to a conference room where we would interrogate the six executives in question. With Jenny's agreement we didn't place an artificial time limit on our interrogations with each man. Hopefully, one or more of them would open up. You never know what clues you may find until you start interrogating people.

Our first interrogee, John Stormer, walked in and sat down. We exchanged pleasantries. I noticed that he didn't smile at all. We agreed that Bobbie would begin the conversation. When questioning men, we've always noticed that they tend to be open with Bobbie. Her intoxicating good looks probably has something to do with that.

"John, have you been to Montauk Point recently?" Bobbie doesn't like slow buildups and prefers to get right to the point like a homing pigeon. Although we knew he had been in Montauk, along with all the others, from the GPS data on their phones, Bobbie wanted to see how open this guy was willing to be.

"Yes, I was there a couple of weeks ago while on vacation."

"And have you ever heard of an organization known as the Committee of Freedom?"

"Yes. It's run by our leader and savior, Chairman Peter Solomon."

Bobbie and I looked at each other. We expected it would take an hour to get to this point. This guy had nothing to hide or didn't think he did. We expected a lot of evasiveness but got none. It was almost as if we were being taunted. Our leader and savior? Holy shit.

"John, what can you tell us about a process known as the Re-Education Program?"

"What do you want to know about it?"

"Can you tell us how the Re-Education Program works and where it's conducted?"

"I have no idea."

Finally, the evasiveness we were expecting. But something about the guy's face told us he wasn't lying. Bobbie and I have become experts over the years at spotting lies. We look for facial tics, eye movements, or a change in voice or posture. But no, this guy seemed to be telling the truth, or at least he *believed* he was telling the truth.

"But John, you went through the program did you not?

"No, I didn't. I'm sure I would remember something like that if I did."

"Did any of your colleagues here at Robot Depot go through the Re-Education Program?"

"Not to my knowledge."

Bobbie nodded to me, indicating that I should take over the questioning. I decided to avoid any discussion of the Re-Education Program since it didn't seem to lead anywhere. I figured it was time to crawl into this guy's head.

"John, before you referred to Peter Solomon—

"That's *Chairman* Peter Solomon."

"Yes, of course, Chairman Peter Solomon. You referred to him as our leader and savior. Why did you say that about him?"

"Because he *is* our leader and savior, yours too."

"Can you describe any of his words or actions that led you to that conclusion?"

"Everything Chairman Solomon says and does convinces me that he is our leader and savior. He has created the New World Order. He has ordered us to abandon our old stupid ways of thinking and follow his leadership in accepting the new reality."

Holy shit. This guy had not only been brainwashed but went

through a few extra cycles of spin dry. Bobbie and I looked at each other and nodded. We decided to end our interview with John, the Robot, Stormer. We spent the next four hours interrogating the other five executives. We were treated to a steady stream of "our leader and savior," "the New World Order," and "the New Reality."

Our final interrogee, Philip McLaughlin, did give us some new information. He remembered going through the Re-Education Program. He described an auditorium filled with about 200 people. He told us that a series of large machines traveled back and forth along tracks on the ceiling, setting off an electronic hum. Attached to each machine was an instrument that looked like a gun barrel and would emit loud clicking sounds as it focused randomly at each member of the audience. He even described the appearance of a huge door that led to a hallway and a series of elevators that would descend deep into the earth and the auditorium.

We left the conference room and went to Jenny Bateman's office as planned. Jenny, always the polite lady, rose to greet us. I could tell from the look on her face that she was dying to hear the results of our interrogations. She reached for a water pitcher and poured us each a glass.

"Jenny, Bobbie and I think of you as a friend, and therefore have a recommendation. We strongly suggest that you fire those assholes immediately. They can do your company an enormous amount of harm, and they may have already done so."

We described our interrogations in detail for Jenny. She sat there shaking her head.

"Do you guys think that one or more of these men had something to do with our robot riot at the Venetian Hotel?"

"Let me put it this way, Jenny, I wouldn't trust these guys with a set of Legos, much less work on the complex engineering your company requires. We're going now, but we hope to see you soon."

"Bob, don't forget about our dinner invitation."

"Oh, right. Bobbie and I would like to invite you to a small dinner party at our house in East Hampton. How about next Friday?"

"I'd love to and I graciously accept. I've heard about your lovely house and I'm dying to see it. Since Mike died my social life has been on hold. I look forward to getting together with my detective pals."

Bobbie and I were happy about our day spent at Robot Depot. The most significant information we gathered was the details on the mysterious Re-Education Program. We'd soon find out how significant that information was.

CHAPTER 23

Bobbie

There's a big tall man walking up to the house," Jane said. "My God, is he handsome."

"And what's my pretty wife doing ogling guys?" Jane's husband Steve said with a laugh as he sat playing with Tilly.

"I'm just reporting the obvious, honey. He's not as handsome as my hubby, but he's definitely a good-looking man."

The doorbell rang and I answered it.

"Hi, Bobbie, how have you been?"

"Rick, great to see you," as I gave him a welcome hug. Bob walked into the room and he and Rick bear-hugged one another. Unlike 1943, in 2019 people exchange hugs, both men and women.

"Jane and Steve," I said, "meet FBI agent Rick Patton, a good friend of ours. We've worked many a case together."

"So, Rick are you still with the FBI field office in Melville?"

"Yes, I was transferred back there just recently after a couple of years in California. I was going to call you, but I was out here to visit my cousin and figured I'd surprise you. I'm glad to see you're here on Long Island."

"Yeah, and it looks like we may spend the rest of our lives here. Do you know much about this quarantine?"

"A bit, but I don't doubt that you and Bob are ahead of us. The BBs don't waste time. We should get together and compare notes. Hey, I've got to run to an appointment. I'll call you soon."

"Hey, Rick, please join us for dinner next Friday."

"Yeah," Bob said. "We've also invited a special guest."

"Shush, Bob. Let's make it a surprise."

Bob shot me a confused look, but didn't press the issue.

After Rick left, Bob said, "Why didn't you want me to tell him about Jenny Bateman?"

"Jenny and Rick are both single and lonely. Who knows, maybe they'll like each other."

"Since when have you become a matchmaker?"

"Yenta could be my middle name. This will be fun."

"Or a disaster."

CHAPTER 24

Bobbie

Tonight, Bob and I are hosting a small dinner party. Jane and Steve will be there, of course as well as our little Tilly. We invited our new friends, Tim Gleason, our time travelling pal from 1943 and his new wife, Becca. She and Tim had a whirlwind romance after Tim intentionally returned to 2019 so he could see her again after a brief, but obviously meaningful, encounter. Bob and I stood up for them when they married three months ago. They're obviously quite in love. Bob and I pulled a few strings and secured Tim a job with the Suffolk County Police Department. Becca still works as an Army officer at Camp Hero in Montauk. They're good people and we're happy to count them as friends. Bob and I seem to have a habit of collecting new friends. Beats stamp collecting.

But what has me excited is that we've invited Jenny Bateman from Robot Depot and Rick Patton, our FBI friend. Maybe I'm crazy, but I'm dying to introduce Jenny and Rick. They're both great people, good looking as hell, and single and lonely. Bob always tells me I'm a hopeless romantic. Maybe he's right.

Rick showed up an hour early at 5 p.m. so he could review with Bob and me our investigations. Jane, our brilliant chef and babysitter, was preparing the dinner. Maybe she can teach me how to cook. Screw it, making reservations is so much easier.

We stood around the kitchen having drinks. I sipped my boring Perrier. My tummy was beginning to show a baby bump, and it will be a few months before I can have a real drink.

At 6 p.m. the doorbell rang. It was Jenny Bateman. I was so excited about introducing her and Rick that I felt as if I was having a bout of morning sickness. I answered the door and escorted Jenny into the kitchen. As usual, she looked lovely, wearing an expensive pale blue Neiman Marcus dress. She also wore navy blue pumps which showed off her long beautiful legs.

She and Rick stared at each other for a few awkward moments and then softly said each other's names. Then they hugged, a bit more than a simple "long-time-no-see" hug. Obviously, they know each other well, or did at one time.

"Rick and I met when he was in charge of the FBI investigation into that terrorist case involving our products," Jenny said, her face wearing a perma-smile.

"Yes, Jenny and I worked quite closely," Rick said, staring at Jenny as he did.

I noticed that they couldn't seem to take their eyes off each other. When Rick mentioned that he and Jenny once worked "quite closely," I could swear I saw sparks fly. I was so happy with their reaction to each other my stomach started to do flips.

I walked over to the bar to help Bob serve a few more drinks. "Holy shit," I whispered. "can you spell the word 'chemistry?' I thought they were going to jump each other. Looks like my Yenta duties have played out well." Bob smiled, pinched me on the ass, and kissed my cheek. I'm not the only romantic in this family.

We sat down to dinner. I placed Jenny and Rick next to each other, and they seemed quite happy with that arrangement. Jane and Steve insisted that they act as waiter and waitress. Our dinner conversation was great, with lots of laughs and storytelling. Jenny and Rick kept stealing glances at each other— long glances, and occasionally whispering. I noticed their hands often touched. It was obvious, at least to me, that those two once felt a relationship brewing, and it seemed that it was brewing once again. They are two great-looking people, no doubt about it. My inner romantic imagined how good looking their kids would be. Shit, there I go again. Soon, no doubt, I'll be helping Jenny pick out china.

Rick told a funny story, or at least he thought it was funny. We all chuckled, except for Jenny, who burst out into hysterical laughter. I don't know if she found the story particularly funny or that she just wanted to send a message to Rick, a message that said she enjoyed being with him. He sure as hell seemed to enjoy being with her. I'm sure they must have taken their eyes off each other occasionally, but if they did, I didn't notice.

Tim and Becca talked nonstop and seemed to be enjoying the party. I'm glad we invited them. We discussed with Tim that he should not bring up time travel, thinking that would totally dominate the conversation.

Jenny and Rick not only couldn't take their eyes off each other but couldn't keep their hands to themselves. They would constantly stroke each other's arms or hold hands.

After dinner wound down, we all stood around exchanging small talk. Jenny took out her cellphone and keyed in some numbers.

"Placing a bet?" I said. She laughed. "I'm just dialing for my Uber."

"Don't be silly," Rick said. "I'll drive you home, Jenny."

In a split-second Jenny immediately cancelled her Uber. "That would be really nice of you, Rick," she said softly, looking at him as if she wanted him for dessert.

Something told me he would do more than drop her off, maybe drop her panties.

Bobbie the Yenta. Yesss!

CHAPTER 25

Bobbie

At 9 a.m. on Saturday morning Jenny Bateman called.

"God bless you, girl. I think I've found a new best friend."

"Rick?"

"No. My new best friend would be you, Bobbie. Rick's more than a friend as I'll explain shortly. I can't get over that you didn't know Rick and I knew one another. I guess it was just good luck that you invited us both. And it definitely *was* good luck. He's the detective who took over the investigation of the murder of my husband. Rick's a hell of an investigator. He knew what evidence to concentrate on, but he also knew what evidence to ignore. I'll tell you more about that the next time I see you, not on the phone. When Mike was killed, I thought my heart would crack into a million pieces. We had a wonderful marriage, just like you and Bob. And suddenly it was over. The more I worked with Rick, the closer I felt to him, and I appreciated not only his professionalism, but the way he comforted me. I was conflicted as hell and blamed my feelings on the phenomenon of rebound. Besides his gorgeous looks, he had a gentle way about him. The more I resisted the idea, the more I realized that a certain chemistry was percolating between us. But then he was reassigned to an FBI unit in California, so nothing happened, although we both wanted something to happen. So, I feel like I've known this guy for a long time. I guess I have. And then my best friend Bobbie Nelson brought us together again."

I started to get choked up. "Oh my God, what a lovely story Jenny. I guess you and Rick shared some sweet nothings when he drove you home."

"Sweet nothings? We exchanged a lot more than sweet nothings. I was going to go for a run this morning, but I'm not sure I can even walk. Oh, my God, did I just say that? Oh, what the hell, girlfriends can confide in each other. Then the most beautiful thing happened a couple of hours ago just as he was leaving. He told me he loved me. I knew it wasn't just passion talking. The look in his face and his gentle touch told me it was the real thing. He just laid his heart bare. And then I told him what I had felt for him a long time ago. I told him that I loved him."

"Holy shit," I said. "You two don't waste time, do you?"

"Hey, Bobbie, we're both 39 and know what we're doing. Something's been missing from my life since Mike died. Last night I realized what was missing. Rick Patton was missing. And because of Detective Yenta Nelson, he's no longer missing. I've found him again."

I was starting to fill up as Jenny told her story. When she said that thanks to me she "found him again," I totally lost it, sobbing tears of joy.

Jenny would later tell me what she had been unable to say on the phone. She mentioned that, during his investigation into the murder of Mike Bateman, Rick knew what evidence to ignore. That confused me. As a detective I never ignore evidence. Turns out, the evidence was quite clear that the lovely, charming Jenny Bateman, personally assassinated the six terrorists responsible for Mike's death. Mike Bateman was brutally murdered by the group of thugs, decapitated with a machete in his car as it was parked in their driveway. Jenny discovered his headless body. Rick told her that he knew he was in love with her as he uncovered the evidence that Jenny killed the terrorists, evidence that he chose to ignore in his report. He said it showed the love she had for her husband, a love that Rick now wants to share.

We planned to meet at Robot Depot and come up with a plan to do something about the Long Island quarantine. Jenny said that she had some ideas involving robots. Jenny is never without ideas. I couldn't wait to meet with the two high-powered lovebirds Monday morning.

CHAPTER 26

Bob

I often think that Bobbie is the most caring person I've ever met. When she told me about her phone conversation with Jenny Bateman and how Bobbie's "Yenta" idea played out so beautifully in bring together two great people, I filled up. She so totally cares about other people. Bobbie, my other half, is also my better half. I love that woman. How can I not?

Bobbie and I arrived at Robot Depot at 9 a.m. for our planned meeting with Jenny Bateman and Rick Patton. Like Bobbie, I was dying to watch the two newly rediscovered lovers in a business setting.

When we walked into Jenny's office, Rick stood and gave Bobbie a bear hug.

"Jenny calls you Bobbie the matchmaker, and I agree. God bless you, Bobbie, for making me the happiest man in the world."

Then Jenny gave Bobbie a hug. Then she and Rick engaged in a hug best described as R-rated. Hey, get a room.

Bobbie and Rick agreed that I would give a summary of where we are in the matter of our strange quarantine. As happy as I was with Bobbie's matchmaking, I was also delighted that we'd be working with a tough and experienced FBI agent like Rick. He's well-known at the NYPD. It's good we'll be working together, because the look on Jenny's face told me that she didn't want him out of her sight.

I told them about our trip to Whitestone where we saw dozens of army tanks and a brigade of soldiers, and about our conversation with the young private who brought us up to speed on the Committee of Freedom. Then I recounted our meeting at the Suffolk County Police Department where we met the under-cover FBI agent who opined that Peter Solomon is the most dangerous man in the world. The most exciting story I had to tell was our trip to Montauk where we time travelled and interrogated that imprisoned sergeant who kept talking about "our leader and savior," Peter Solomon, and the New World Order. But the key to everything so far was our interrogation of the strange Robot Depot executives. I asked Bobbie to talk about that since she did most of the interrogating.

"Bob and I were blown away with our interrogation of your six brainwashed executives. They all kept on with the now familiar 'leader and savior' bullshit and the 'New World Order.' But the last guy we drilled gave us something important. He told us where the strange Re-Education Project is located in Montauk, and even gave us directions on how to get there."

"I'm not sure that gets you very far, Bobbie," Rick Patton said. "What will you do, knock on the door and say, 'Hi, we're with the NYPD and we have a few questions?' I don't think you'll get very far, and I think you'll be putting yourselves in serious danger."

"That's where I come in," Jenny said, "or more accurately, that's where Robot Depot comes in."

She pressed her intercom and said, "Phil, please bring us an R259."

Handsome Phil, who is a life-sized robot, came in with a small instrument that looked like a flashlight with a large screw-like appendage at the top, and bulldozer-like tracks on the bottom. Phil then walked back out and returned with a large piece of a tree trunk.

He placed the tree trunk on the floor and the R259 a few feet in front of it. Jenny aimed a remote at the device and it rolled on its tracks toward the tree trunk. About two inches before the trunk, the R259 swiveled to a horizontal position and bore a hole in the wood, sliding inside the hole it just made. It hardly made a sound, just a very slight whirring noise, even as the device bored a hole in the trunk. Jenny then pressed another button on the remote and the R259 reemerged from the tunnel it had just made. She then pressed another button and a projector screen came down from the ceiling. Projected on the screen was a perfectly lit view of the inside of the tree trunk.

"This thing is as top secret as top secret gets," Jenny said. "We designed this for the US Army and it's fully operational. So, here's the plan. We place an R259 a couple of hundred feet from the entrance to the building you want access to. It has a tracking mechanism so we can visually follow it by looking at a screen. The plan is to bore through a wall in the building and then go vertical and descend to the basement where we hope the auditorium is located. We think we have a pretty good idea where the auditorium is because one of our executives who Bob and Bobbie interrogated described the location. The device is designed to go through sub floors so the chance of someone seeing it is minimal. Once the top two inches are through the floor it can snap photos galore. It even has a powerful listening and recording device. If it works, we will have a visual and auditory experience of a Re-Education Project seminar."

We were, quite simply, stunned. My God, Robot Depot is a lot more than automatic vacuum cleaners.

'What if somebody sees the device as it emerges from a floor or wall?" Bobbie said. She always thinks 10 moves ahead.

"The device is almost silent as you probably have noticed. Also, it has sensor cells that can detect footsteps. Because it's a foregone conclusion that you can't get a human being to spy on that place, the R259 is our best shot."

"Do I know how to pick girlfriends or not," Rick said as he reached over and stroked Jenny's face. She grabbed his hand, smiled at him, and kissed it. He kept staring into Jenny's eyes as she spoke. I almost expected Jenny to call a 45-minute break so she and Rick could go into "executive session" in her back office. My Bobbie, the Yenta, did a great job bringing these two together.

I was trying to think positively. That R259 device is incredible, and Jenny is probably right, It's our best shot. But even if the thing works as planned, we would still have nothing more than a video of a seminar. The cooperative executive from Robot Depot was helpful, but he didn't give us an enormous amount of detail about what happens at a Re-Education Project seminar. So, we're stuck with a robot, an amazing robot to be sure, but still, a robot.

CHAPTER 27

Bobbie

Bob and I decided to give Jane a break from her self-appointed cooking duties and we invited her to join us for lunch at John Papas Café along with Steve and Tilly. I wondered if we'd ever get to eat again at one of Manhattan's great restaurants.

"Bob, am I seeing things? That looks like Bennie Weinberg."

"That's definitely, Bennie, hon, and his wife, Maggie. Why don't you invite them to eat with us?"

I walked over to their table. Bennie, a good friend, stood and gave me a hug as did Maggie. Dr. Benjamin Weinberg is a psychiatrist as well as a detective first grade with the NYPD. His nickname is Bennie the Bullshit Detector. He's a favorite with prosecutors because he has an uncanny ability to spot lies on the witness stand. He's also a damn good detective. He graduated from Harvard Medical School, and is one of the smartest people I've ever met, even though he has the foul mouth of a NYPD cop. He often jokes that he broke his mother's heart when he opted to become a cop. And when he showed her a joke business card that read "Bennie the

Bullshit Detector," he thought she'd disown him. Bennie's a good-looking man, 5'10 in height, somewhat overweight, which he masks by wearing expensive designer clothes. He's going bald, and I've always been impressed that he doesn't mask it with a comb-over. Maggie, whom we've met many times, is a pretty petite woman with a great figure and a wild shock of red hair. She's a professor of criminology at NYU and has been deputized as a NYPD detective often. He and Maggie joined us at our table.

"Maggie and I came out here to spend a weekend at the Montauk Manor, one of our favorite resorts, just before the quarantine. I figured you two were in Manhattan and I tried to look up your phone number out here, but of course it's unlisted. Hey, we've got a lot to talk about. How about we go to your house after lunch?"

After lunch, we drove to our house with Bennie and Maggie following us. When we pulled into the driveway, Maggie, the Golden Retriever from next door, came bounding up to us.

"What an adorable dog," Maggie Weinberg said. "What's her name?"

"Uh, Fido," I said.

We met in the office next to our suite on the second floor. Jane and Steve get it. They know that some of our work is and must be secret. A former Army Ranger lieutenant, Steve understands the doctrine of "need to know."

"Holy shit," Bennie yelled with his usual cop mouth, "this house is like a friggin resort. Looks like you guys enjoy your book royalties."

Bennie is also a best-selling author. I chuckled at his comment about our money, because Bennie and Maggie are quite loaded.

"I assume we're free to speak with Maggie here," I said.

"Yeah, Maggie is my detective partner half the time and she

definitely has a need to know. So, what can you guys tell me about this cluster fuck we find ourselves in? I'm especially interested in the rumors I've heard about a thing called the Re-Education Project, which I've heard is run out of somewhere in Montauk Point."

"Well, we know where it is, and most importantly we've found a way that we may be able to infiltrate and actually see a video recording of an actual re-education group of seminars. Yesterday we met with Jenny Bateman, CEO of Robot Depot. They've invented a device that can tunnel under the earth and drill through walls. The robot then can record anything it sees. The device has the charming name R259."

I couldn't resist telling Bennie and Maggie about my matchmaking talents.

"I know Rick Patton well," Bennie said. "He's one hell of a fine FBI agent. I think it's great that he'll be working with you. And from what you just said about bringing him and Jenny Bateman together, he owes you one."

We filled Ben and Maggie in on all the details we knew about the R259.

"That sounds great," Bennie said, "but how can we interpret what we're looking at?"

"You hit the problem on the head, Bennie, which doesn't surprise me. But as of right now this little robot is the only shot we have about learning more about the Re-Education Project. We got some information from an executive at Robot Depot, but not much."

The phone rang. I looked at caller ID and saw that it was Commissioner Mike Townsend.

"I better take this. It's the Suffolk County Police Commissioner."

CHAPTER 28

Bobbie

I've got a resister," Mike Townsend said.

"That's nice, Mike. Now try speaking English."

"I don't want to go into detail over the phone. How soon can you get here?"

"We'll be there in 45 minutes. You'll be delighted to know that none other than Bennie Weinberg will be with us. I'm sure you know about Bennie."

"Of course, I know about Bennie Weinberg. The man is a law enforcement legend. He's the perfect guy to be in on this meeting. I look forward to meeting him personally."

"His wife and partner, Maggie, will be with us. She's a provisional detective with the NYPD as well as a professor of criminology, so don't worry about security clearances."

We pulled up to the SCPD at 2:30. A uniformed cop escorted us to Mike's office. We introduced Bennie and Maggie.

"What an honor to meet you, Dr. Weinberg. I've read all of your books."

"Please, the name's Bennie."

"As in Bennie the Bullshit Detector?" Mike said, laughing.

"The one and only."

I figured I'd get right to the point. "So, what's this thing about you having a *resister*, whatever that means?"

"We've found a man who went through the Re-Education Program but wasn't re-educated. He's completely normal and knows every detail about the Re-Education Project."

Oh, my God, if we combine this "resister" with the tunneling robot from Robot Depot we could be ready to turn a corner. Bob and I then brought Mike up to speed on the ground-breaking tunneling robot, the R259. We all agreed that the R259 could give us the basics, but this resister guy can interpret what we'll be looking at.

"This man could be exactly who we're looking for," Maggie said.

"What's his name and when will he be here?"

"His name is Stan Crowley and he'll be here in five minutes. We're putting him up at headquarters because obviously we can't risk losing this guy. He's a detective, you'll be happy to know, with the NYPD. He works out of Queens."

Neither Bob nor I knew the guy, but that's okay. We're used to working with detectives.

Mike's assistant led Stan Crowley into the office. Bob and I immediately recognized him from working various crime scenes, although we had never met him personally.

"Wow, I get to meet the famous BBs, not to mention Doctor

Weinberg. My lucky day."

We spent a few minutes exchanging pleasantries. It's been my experience, that even if you have major things to talk about, the best way to get there is to get to know the people you're dealing with on a personal basis.

"Stan, please lay out for us in detail your experience with this thing called the Re-Education Project," Mike said.

"For openers, I was kidnapped as I was about to get into my car in Queens. Very slick operators, those people. I was no sooner in their car when they put a tissue over my face, apparently intending to sedate me with what I assume was something like Ambien. I assumed it was Ambien because it had no effect on me at all. I'm immune to the drug, have been all my life. If I need a sleeping pill I go for a martini. But I figured I'd better play along with the game, so I faked that I was stoned. An hour and a half later we pulled into Camp Hero in Montauk. I was escorted to an area where about 200 people were gathered. I was still faking being under the influence. The others weren't faking—they were stoned. We were led through a large steel door into a long hallway. All of us were herded down the hall to a group of elevators and we were told to get in. We descended exactly six floors and got off. We were escorted down the hall to an auditorium."

"Stan, can you describe where the auditorium is located?" I asked.

"Yes, it's on the bottom floor of the northwest side of the building. I have a memory like an elephant and my detective training always results in my subconsciously orienting myself to my surroundings. When we were seated a group of people in strange uniforms walked among us with cups of liquid on trays. I sniffed at the liquid and immediately realized it was good old Ambien, so I didn't resist drinking it. I figured they thought of it as a booster shot. A lovely classical music piece played over the speakers in the auditorium.

I think it was from Bach, one of his Partitas. The atmosphere was classy. Then it started to get weird. The curtains on the stage parted, revealing a large movie screen. A video played. A guy introduced himself as Peter Solomon, Chairman of that outfit called the Committee of Freedom. Every day, as the others in my group became 're-educated,' they kept referring to that creep Solomon as 'our leader and savior.' How fucking weird is that? They also kept babbling on about a thing called 'the New World Order.' Bizarre shit I tell you."

"What happened from day to day, Stan?" I asked.

"Beginning with the first hour right after the introductory video, huge instruments began crossing the ceiling on an elaborate track system in an apparent random pattern. From each device poked a long pipe, looking like the barrel of a gun. I heard a constant electronic hum, which was punctuated by loud clicking sounds as the instruments travelled along the ceiling. I noticed that the barrels pointed to random members of the audience. As I heard the clicking sounds, I saw an occasional person twitch as if he'd been struck by something. As the instruments travelled along the ceiling, I heard odd messages being recited, stuff like, 'Chairman Solomon is your leader and savior,' or 'abandon your old way of thinking and embrace the New World Order.' Totally weird shit."

"Did you feel anything strike you?" Bennie asked.

"It was almost imperceptible, but I did feel occasional puffs of air. I know this may sound odd, but I think my immunity to Ambien somehow prevented me from turning into a zombie like the others. Does that make any sense at all, Dr. Bennie?"

"Yes, it does make sense, Stan. Immunity, as you call it, to Ambien is extremely rare. In the few cases I've studied, the immune person is also resistant to loud and regular noises. These procedures, conducted over five days, combined with the Ambien, seems to be the way people's minds are controlled. What you've just described is a form of mass hypnosis, aided by the Ambien. If this line of inquiry is on target, I have a hunch that we may be able to find a cure to the re-education."

It was as if a bomb just went off in the room. Holy shit, a cure?

"Please explain, Ben," Commissioner Mike said, wiping some perspiration from his forehead.

"There is an aerosol spray called Torlazine that can counteract the effects of Ambien, and also the effects of hypnosis. It's sort of like immunizing a person after the fact. If I'm right about what I'm speculating, we can drastically reduce the zombie population that came through the Re-Education Program. Commissioner Mike, didn't you tell me that you have a few officers here at the SCPD who have apparently gone through re-education?"

"Yes, we have three such individuals. All three are here at headquarters under temporary lockdown until we can figure out what to do with them."

"You have an infirmary here at police headquarters, yes?" Bennie said.

"We do, but I don't know if we stock that Torlazine stuff."

"It's a common drug and quite safe. It's also cheap. I'm going to the infirmary now and see if they stock it. I'd appreciate it if you'd call the infirmary to give me an introduction and let them know I'm on my way. I'll be back in a few minutes."

Five minutes went by and Bennie came back to the office with a huge smile on his face. He held up a small spray bottle.

"Folks, allow me to introduce you to Torlazine, the anti-Ambien. Mike, I recommend that we try this on one of the strange-acting cops in the lockdown. He'll be in no danger at all. I want to try this on him so I can demonstrate to all of you what this drug can do."

"Fred, bring officer John Brand in here would you. Keep him in handcuffs," Mike said to his assistant.

Mike turned to us and said, "Officer Brand is a total nut case. All he does is talk about our leader and savior and the New World Order."

A couple of minutes later, Fred walked in with Officer Brand, who was in handcuffs.

"Have a seat, John," Mike said. "How have you been feeling?"

"I'm feeling confident about the coming New World Order."

"Close your eyes for a moment, John." He did as Bennie reached over and sprayed the substance into Brand's face.

He sat still for about a minute, his eyes still shut. Then he shook his head and opened his eyes.

"What happened? Did I pass out or something? Good afternoon, Commissioner. Can you please tell me why I'm here?"

"We have a few questions for you, John. First, do you recognize the name Peter Solomon?"

"Yeah, isn't he that nut job who claims that he's the chairman of that strange outfit, the Committee of Freedom?"

"Do you recall seeing him recently?"

"I remember seeing him in a video. He was spouting a lot of strange bullshit."

"Do you recall hearing about a thing called the New World Order?"

"Sounds familiar, but the only order I'm thinking about is a cheeseburger. I haven't had lunch yet and I'm starving."

"John, we're going to take a break and leave you here with this gentleman, Dr. Bennie Weinberg. He's a detective with the NYPD and is also a psychiatrist. You've been acting a bit strangely lately, and Dr. Ben is going to have a chat with you. I'll order lunch brought to you. What would you like?"

"Double cheeseburger, fries, cole slaw, and a Diet Coke."

The rest of us adjourned to a nearby conference room, leaving Officer Brand in the good hands of Bennie Weinberg. Bennie asked if Stan Crowley could remain in the room to offer technical advice.

"As a detective, I love it when we achieve a breakthrough, which I think we've just seen," I said. "Now that Bennie the Bullshit Detector is on the case, I think we'll see more."

"Give Bennie a few minutes or so and we'll have a prognosis we can take to the bank," Maggie Weinberg said. Maggie's proud of her brilliant husband and isn't hesitant to brag.

Thirty-five minutes later Bennie and Stan Crowley walked into the conference room. Officer Brand remained in the commissioner's office with Mike's aide sitting next to him. Technically he was still under arrest until Mike Townsend sets him free.

"So, here's my diagnosis," Bennie said. "That young officer is as mentally healthy as the rest of us. I put him through my advanced bullshit detecting analysis. Thanks to Torlazine, he has been *un-re-educated*. He's still a bit confused, having come out of his strange mindset in the commissioner's office, but he's back among the living. I told him all about what he'd been through, with Stan Crowley weighing in. I recommend that he resume his patrol duties immediately, Mike. He's no longer a New World Order zombie."

"Commissioner," his secretary Grace Morgan said. "The weather reports say that we're going to get clipped by the tail end of that hurricane. I recommend that people go to where they need to be. It's not supposed to get bad for another couple of hours."

"Bennie, why don't you and Maggie plan to stay at our house tonight. God knows we have plenty of room. Also, Jane, our wonderful governess, is a fabulous cook."

"Bobbie, God bless you. We had planned to go hiking along the vineyards this afternoon, so we have a change of clothes with us in the car. Nothing like riding out a storm with good friends in a beautiful mansion."

Even after a great day like today, we all knew there were more storms ahead.

CHAPTER 29

Peter Solomon met with his aide, Gloria Wetherill on the deck outside his office overlooking Lake Utah. The air temperature was warm at 75 degrees and it was drizzling. They sat under the overhang on the huge dock. Gloria wore a miniskirt and a blouse with the top two buttons open, revealing a striking view of her ample breasts. No doubt about it, Solomon thought, this 32-year-old woman is sexually attractive. Solomon knew exactly what Gloria was doing. She was trying to attract him, to gain control over what relationship they had. He had slept with her a few times, and enjoyed it. Actually, it was the best sex Solomon had in a long time. The intimacy between him and his five ex-wives never did it for him. Too bad they all passed away at a young age. Solomon had to laugh at Gloria's overt attempts to get control over him. Nobody gets control over Peter Solomon, he thought. But for fun, he may let her think she was getting to him.

They sat in two large comfortable chairs at a small coffee table. It was lunchtime, and two other aides brought food to the table, an assortment of chicken slices, raw vegetables and salads. Nothing elaborate, but that's okay, Peter Solomon liked to keep some things simple. Some things.

Gloria crossed her beautiful bare legs as she bit into a piece of celery, looking dreamily into his eyes. Yes, he thought, she's definitely looking for the upper hand.

"This meeting will begin with a discussion of our Re-Education Program, Gloria, and then we will talk about the political landscape," he said, as he poured them each an iced tea. "I trust that you have good news for me."

"Yes, excellent news, Mr. Chairman. As you ordered, we are introducing groups to the program by category. To date we have had three law enforcement contingents, four military, five journalism groups, one corporate, including Robot Depot, and the most recent were officials with the United States Department of State." She handed him a file of brief documents, making sure to give him a good view of her voluptuous breasts as she bent over to hand them to him. "The State Department officials are proving especially valuable. Soon the entire federal government will be infiltrated by our people. Whoever enters the program at the beginning of the week is a valuable ally of ours at the end of the week. Gradually, we are changing Americans into citizens of the Committee of Freedom."

Solomon smiled.

She kicked off her shoes and perched her pretty bare feet on another chair. She noticed Peter Solomon staring at her suntanned legs. She knew that Solomon liked a relaxed atmosphere when discussing important matters, and what Solomon liked, she intended to provide.

"How many people have gone through the Re-Education program, Gloria?"

"Just under 20,000, sir, going back to the beginning of the program, adjusted of course for those who've passed away, all from the various groups I discussed. Our carpenters are putting the finishing touches on the second building which will house another auditorium as we speak. It should be operational, including the re-education equipment, within three weeks. Then we can increase the classes to over 500 per week."

"Has there been any resistance?"

"Very little, and mostly vocal not physical. The sedatives we give the candidates take care of that."

Solomon lit a cigarette, took a deep drag, and exhaled the smoke. He did not offer one to Gloria.

"Let's discuss our political operation, Gloria. Our nominating convention is coming up soon."

"We have political operations set up in all key states, Mr. Chairman, and will soon have organizations in all 50 states. I'm pleased to say that all our operatives view you as our leader and savior. I know *I* do." She had been practicing in front of a mirror how to strike an "alluring" pose. She did just that as she referred to him as her leader and savior. She winked at him. Shit, I'm making this too obvious. Slow down and play it cool.

It began to rain heavily, forcing them to speak loudly to be heard.

"Let's continue our meeting upstairs in my private office, Gloria, free from the distraction of the rain."

They took an elevator to Solomon's private office, which included a king-sized bed. He walked into the kitchen to get a pitcher of water. When he returned to the room, Gloria had already removed her top and skirt, leaving her standing there in nothing but a thong, her firm breasts signaling welcome.

Yes, Gloria thinks she can control me, the naïve kid. But it does open the opportunity for a valuable release from stress. Quite a release.

CHAPTER 30

Good evening, ladies and gentlemen and welcome to *CBS World News Tonight.* I'm your host, George Stephanopoulos. We depart from our normal pattern of interviewing people tonight, and bring you two gentlemen who are often opponents, Roger Jones, Chairman of the Democratic National Committee, and Blake Andrews, Chairman of the Republican National Committee.

"Recently our country has been witness to a strange phenomenon. Although the Nominating Conventions are only 10 months away, neither major party has put together a slate of candidates, most especially, candidates for the office of President of the United States. The only man in the news as a serious candidate is none other than the enigmatic Peter Solomon, Chairman of the new political party known as the Committee of Freedom.

"Roger, I'll start with you. Why haven't the Democrats put up even a single potential candidate this close to the nominating convention?"

"George, we have quite a few people who have expressed interest in running. The field just hasn't taken shape yet. There is plenty of time."

"I question your statement that there is plenty of time. With only 10 months out we would expect to see massive fundraising and a constant barrage of TV commercials touting various candidates. It's as if there's a reluctance among your people. I'll now address my identical question to Blake Andrews. Blake, why haven't the Republicans fielded even one candidate yet? Something tells me you're going to repeat what Roger just said."

"George, on both sides of the aisle, sometimes the field is crowded with candidates, and sometimes it's sparse."

"Sparse? Zero is less than sparse. It almost seems that you guys are conceding the next presidential race to a man and a party who few people know anything about. I'm going to say something that I know will be controversial, but it appears that people are afraid to run against Peter Solomon and the Committee of Freedom. Can I be right? Are your people afraid to run against this guy?"

"Fear?" Blake Andrews said. "Why would anybody be afraid to run a campaign against Peter Solomon?"

"You tell me."

CHAPTER 31

Bob

Bobbie and I had just pulled up to Robot Depot headquarters in Hauppauge. Bennie and Maggie were with us, having stayed overnight at our place to weather the storm. Because the house is on the water, we were careful to install heavy storm windows throughout. They loved their room and couldn't stop talking about it. It's a full bedroom suite including two bathrooms overlooking Georgica Pond. The day began with bright sun, a welcome change from the storm the night before. None of us had gotten much sleep because of the hurricane force winds. I was happy to see that we hadn't sustained any serious damage. Half the pool furnaiture was now in the pool, which was no problem. A large tree had fallen and half of it was lying in Georgica Pond.

———

An hour later we walked into Jenny Bateman's office, escorted by Phil the robot. Agent Rick Patton was already there with Jenny. I noticed that Jenny's normal carefully coiffed hair was a bit undone, as if she had just engaged in some rigorous physical activity. She and Rick were sitting next to each other at the conference table, with less than a zillionth of a centimeter between them. When they noticed us they hurriedly released each other's hand. Lovebirds.

Bobbie and I had planned to insert the tunneling robot at Camp Hero, but we all agreed that our faces were too well-known and we would risk blowing our cover. Jenny assigned three of her engineers to do the planting, along with Detective Stan Crowley, the resister, the man who went through the re-education program but was not re-educated. Stan knew Camp Hero well, having gone through the re-education program without losing his mind. We watched what was happening on a large screen in Jenny's office. She had ordered bagels, lox, and cream cheese to quiet our growling stomachs. Jenny prepared a plate for Rick and gently pushed it in front of him, their eyes locked together. Jenny winked as she blew him a kiss. Wow. When Bobbie nails a project, she nails it.

If this plan worked, we would have a visual of the re-education auditorium itself, with Bennie and Stan Crowley there to do the analyzing. All our eyes were trained on the viewing screen in Jenny's office, although Rick's and Jenny's eyes often meandered to each other.

As the R259 burrowed into the ground 100 feet from the entrance doors, there wasn't much we could see, even though there was a powerful light on the tip of the device. Not much to see when you're tunneling under dirt, however. The device came to a sudden stop, telling us that it had found the first wall. We heard a barely audible whirring sound as it tunneled through. After 25 minutes of straight travelling, the machine went vertical and the R259 suddenly tunneled up and through a floor. Oh, my God, it's inside the auditorium. Stan Crowley obviously remembered his directions well. As the R259 swiveled its camera, we could see the instruments along the ceiling that Crowley had described as the scanning devices that pointed their barrels at peoples' heads and emitted loud clicking sounds. He called us from his secure cellphone and pointed out the details to us as he lay in the bushes outside the building viewing the scene on his iPad. Jenny put him on speaker and linked the connection through a loudspeaker on her desk. A seminar had just begun, and we could see people walking amidst the audience administering a clear liquid in plastic cups.

"An extra dose of Ambien no doubt," Bennie said.

We watched the screen in front of the auditorium as Peter Solomon sang the praises of the Committee of Freedom and welcomed people to accept the New World Order and to abandon their old way of thinking. I had a hard time believing that we were inside—deep inside.

Once Solomon's video ended, Stan Crowley told us to listen for the humming sound. There it was. The R259 pointed its camera up to the ceiling as the large devices with what looked like gun barrels began to move. "Now listen for the clicks," Crowley said.

The humming and clicking were punctuated by a steady drumbeat of words from someone through the speakers. There was no inflection in the man's voice, just the constant rhythmic cadence of words for those being re-educated. "Peter Solomon is your leader and savior," "Welcome to the New World Order," "Abandon your old ways of thinking."

After four hours, the seminar came to an end as announced by a man on the stage. He spoke softly so as to not burden the participants with words other than the creepy propaganda they were pounded with. We then saw a group of men and women circulate through the crowd with hand-held recording devices. From the questions they asked, it was obvious that they were trying to assess the results of the re-education so far.

We heard Stan Crowley's voice over the speaker. "What you just saw is exactly what goes on for five days straight. I think the R259 has done its work. I don't think we should take any further chances with the robot and I recommend that we retrieve it now."

Jenny agreed and told her lead engineer to retrieve the R259. The robot sank into the tunnel it had just created and began its journey back to the Robot Depot engineers waiting outside the building.

"Well, Bennie," I said. "have you come to any conclusions?"

"I certainly have. What we just saw was hypnosis, plain and simple. The constant clicking sounds from those devices along the ceiling are typical of a hypnotic procedure. Often a hypnotist will use a metronome with its monotonous sounds to help induce a trance. And, aided by the Ambien, it results in a permanent state of mind altered behavior—until Torlazine is administered. Folks, we've found the Rosetta Stone, the cure to Solomon's Re-Education."

"So, Bennie, how do you recommend we go about administering the Torlazine to those affected?" Bobbie asked.

"It begins with detective work, plain and simple. CIA, FBI, NYPD and other law enforcement agencies across the country will be involved. We need to assign insiders to find out who has gone through re-education. Then it's a simple matter of spraying them with Torlazine. It shouldn't be too difficult, although it will take a lot of manpower. Just like the folks here at Robot Depot realized that some of their people were acting weird and spouting Committee of Freedom propaganda, other organizations will realize the same thing. Just track 'em down and administer a spray. But I repeat, it's going to take a lot of manpower, combined with discipline and secrecy. I see this as a clandestine military campaign, and I think I know the perfect guy to lead the operation."

CHAPTER 32

Bob

Stan Crowley walked into the room, having just gotten back from Montauk.

"So, Bennie, who is this military leader who you see heading up this operation?" Bobbie said as she poured herself and me a glass of water.

"Ever hear of Marine General Michael Bennet?"

"Bennie, are you serious?" I said. "I had no idea that General Mike was here on Long Island."

"Do you know him, Bob?"

"Know him? He was my commanding officer when I headed that rifle company in Iraq. I've also served on his staff. We've since become good friends. General Mike worked closely with the NYPD when that weird outfit headed by Antonio Martin began attacking American college campuses. You're right, Bennie, Mike would be the perfect man to head up this operation."

"And General Bennet is Bob's biggest fan," Bobbie said. "The first time I met him, he wouldn't shut up about my handsome hubby's heroics in Iraq. The general personally decorated Bob with the Bronze Star for valor."

Bobbie loves to flatter me, but sometimes it's embarrassing.

"Where's he located, Bennie?"

"He's come out of retirement and temporarily commands the Marine Corps office in Amityville, just a few miles from here. I'm sure the Joint Chiefs have bigger plans for him. Since you know him well, Bob, why don't you give him a call so we can get together."

I Googled the Amityville Marine Corps office and called. I spoke to a young lieutenant, General Mike's aide. She said he was in a meeting but would cut in and ask if he'd be available for a meeting.

"Wow, the general is obviously quite fond of you, Detective," she said less than a minute later. "He immediately said yes. His meeting should be over in a half hour and he looks forward to seeing you."

25 minutes later, we pulled up to the Marine Corps building in Amityville. The structure was surprisingly small. Obviously, this is only a temporary assignment for the general. We were escorted into his office by a Marine corporal armed with an M16 and a sidearm. General Mike was standing by the window in his office. He likes to stand. If you were casting an actor to play a Marine Corps general for a movie, you couldn't go wrong to base him on General Mike. He's a tall man, at 6'5" and carries himself like the disciplined warrior he once was. He's 55 years old but looks much younger. His short-cropped brown hair was streaked with gray. When he looks at you with his steel blue eyes, you feel compelled to salute. I know I did. The walls of the small office were decorated with photos of General Mike in action. I noticed one photo of him standing next to me in Iraq.

He walked across the room in three long strides. "Great to see you again, Captain Bob," he said as he wrapped me in a friendly headlock. "And it's a pleasure to see you too, Bobbie. My God, you get more beautiful every time I see you." He leaned over and kissed her hand. General Mike is a courteous gentleman as well as a tough-as-nails warrior. I introduced Bennie and Maggie Weinberg. The general had spoken to Bennie on occasion but had never met him in person.

General Mike immediately took command of the meeting, which came second nature to him.

"I don't know if you and your wife know Bob well, Bennie, but I'm here to tell you that this handsome young detective was one of the hardest charging grunts under my command. I decorated him with the Bronze Star for heroism, but I tried to convince the higher ups to make it the Navy Cross. Bob risked his life and personally intervened to stop his rifle company from being overrun. I'm happy to see Bob is on Long Island, because the days ahead of us are going to require Bob's kind of courage—a lot of it."

"General Mike, I'm surprised to see you in such a small command for a four-star general."

"That's because we're stuck here on Long Island. President Fenton called me yesterday to tell me that he's appointing me Commandant of the Marine Corps. But my office will be in Washington, not here on Long Island. I'll take full command when we're able to get off this island."

Wow, nothing less than Commandant of the Marine Corps. Although I wasn't in uniform, I stood and saluted him. Bobbie gave him a hug. General Mike will soon be the highest-ranking officer in the Corps. Bennie and Maggie shook his hand.

Hats off to Bennie for picking the right guy.

"Hey, you folks called to see me, so I'll keep my mouth shut, which isn't easy. So, what's on your mind?"

"General, I don't know how much you've learned about the Committee of Freedom, which is the equivalent of a foreign invasion force. Let me fill you in on some amazing things we've discovered in the past few days."

The four of us then brought General Mike up to date on what we'd learned about Peter Solomon and the Committee of Freedom, saving the most significant part for last.

"The most important thing we've learned concerns a process called the Re-Education Project. Have you heard about it, sir?"

"Yes, I've heard about it from a lot of my sources, but I can't say I know a lot of detail, other than it has something to do with Montauk Point."

"Bennie, why don't you tell General Mike everything we've learned. You know more about it than anybody."

"To get right to the point, General," Bennie said, "the enemy—and, yes, that's how we should think about the Committee of Freedom—the enemy, has discovered a method of mass hypnosis. Using a robotic tunneling device, we've seen the way the system works, and we also have on our side a man who went through the process but wasn't affected by it. The subjects are led into an auditorium six levels underground near Camp Hero in Montauk. They are administered large doses of Ambien and subjected to hypnotic procedures for four hours a day for five days. The result is that they go from being ordinary human beings to willing subjects of the Committee of Freedom. They are sent to the re-education program in groups of 200 according to category. The categories, as we've learned so far, are law enforcement, military, journalism, private corporations, and government."

"I believe I've met one of these re-educated people," General Mike said. "Staff Sergeant Mulally was stationed here. Suddenly we noticed that he began babbling nonsense about 'our leader and savior, Peter Solomon,' and he also talked constantly about something called 'the New World Order.' I had him arrested and placed in the brig. He's still there."

"General, I would like to show you a brief demonstration that will explain exactly why we wanted to see you." Bennie said. "May I request that Sergeant Mullaly be brought here to our meeting?"

General Mike buzzed his aide and ordered that Mullaly be brought to his office.

Sergeant Mullaly wore combat fatigues. I noticed that he was quite thin, and his face almost expressionless. The aide seated him at the conference table across from the general. General Mike nodded to Bennie to let him know it was his show.

"Sergeant, can you tell us anything about the Committee of Freedom?" Bennie said.

"Yes, it's the organization run by our leader and savior, Chairman Peter Solomon. It represents the New World Order."

Bennie lifted the spray bottle and squeezed a small cloud of Torlazine into the sergeant's face.

He wiped his nose with a tissue and sat still, looking confused.

"Good afternoon, General. May I ask what I'm doing here?" Sergeant Mullaly said after two minutes.

"I'm going to repeat my question, sergeant" Bennie said. "what can you tell us about the Committee of Freedom?"

"Isn't that the weird organization run by that maniac Peter Solomon?" Sergeant Mullaly said. "I've heard that they keep talking about some New World Order and other assorted crap. They're behind this strange Long Island quarantine, I've been told."

"How do you feel right now, Sergeant?" General Mike said.

"Tired and confused, Sir."

"Lieutenant, bring Sergeant Mullaly to one of the empty private rooms upstairs, not to the brig. Stay outside his room while the sergeant sleeps. Get some rest, Sergeant. We'll talk again soon."

"Okay, folks. Can anybody tell me what the hell just happened?" General Mike said.

"General, you just saw the cure for the Committee of Freedom hypnosis, which they call the Re-Education Program," Bennie said. "The bottle that I sprayed into the sergeant's face contains Torlazine, a cheap and harmless antidote to Ambien, the drug that enables the hypnosis. It works a short time after being sprayed. Our objective is simple—to identify any person who has gone through re-education and spray the Torlazine into his or her face. The simple part is spraying the substance. The complicated part is finding the subjects. That's where you come in, General—hopefully. With your promotion to Commandant of the Marine Corps, I believe you're the perfect man to deliver us from this madness."

"I accept your challenge, on one condition. I want Captain Bob over here to be my second in command, and that the rest of you folks serve on the committee. Bob, I'm hereby giving you a field appointment as an active duty captain in the United States Marine Corps, an action I'm empowered to take in wartime, and we sure as hell are at war. This operation needs to be absolutely top secret. If word gets out our cover is blown. That's why I want you as my second in command, Bob. Nobody gets the job done like you."

Bobbie squeezed my hand and blew me a kiss.

"I have some major logistical concerns" the general said. "I can't wrap my head around the idea of a bunch of soldiers just walking up to people and spraying that stuff into their faces. Some people are bound to put up a fight. Is there a way to put large quantities of that stuff into canisters like tear gas or dropping it from airplanes such as they do with forest fires? How about putting it into the ventilation systems in buildings. Because the Torlazine is harmless, we don't have to worry about it getting into the wrong faces."

"It's worth a try, General," Bennie said. "We don't have solid statistics on how much Torlazine is needed, but I can't see a problem with giving mass spraying a shot. I have a good friend who's a high official with the FDA. I'll ask him if he can intercede with the manufacturer and ramp up production of Torlazine."

"Well, here's a big question," General Mike said, "one which I'm not sure you can provide an answer. But it's the most important question. How many living human beings out there are what you people referred to as re-educated zombies? Has anybody done some calculating?"

"I'm pretty good at math, General, but Bob is amazing," Bobbie said. "Both of us have taken advanced courses over the years on statistical analysis. Bob, honey, I mean Captain, why don't you take it from here?"

"We've come up with an algorithm after a ton of statistical analysis. We know how many people went through the program in the early days from our time travel visit to Camp Hero in 1943. We also have a lot of up-to-date information based largely on what Detective Crowley told us. Without boring you with the details, Bobbie and I have concluded that, adjusting for deaths based on normal life expectancy, that an average of 5 people a week have gone through the Re-

Education Program since 1943. From there the math gets simple.

Multiply the number of weeks since 1943 times five. To date just shy of 20,000 people have been re-educated."

"Dear God," General Mike said. "That's a lot of zombies. So, there are 20,000 people from all walks of life, including journalism, government, and the military. That explains why so many phone calls are answered by strangers. Re-Educated robots are manning the phones. Finding them will be quite a challenge. Any recommendations as to where we should start, Captain Bob?"

"The western shore of Long Island, specifically every bridge and tunnel leading off the Island," I said. "Bobbie and I told you about our experience at the Whitestone Bridge. Those soldiers need to have their faces sprayed. The sooner we return the occupying troops to normal lives, the sooner we can end this quarantine."

CHAPTER 33

Bobbie

On Tuesday evening, Jenny Bateman called. Over the past few weeks we had become fast friends, I think in no small part because I facilitated the rekindling of her relationship with Rick Patton. Bob and I love to meet with them, if only to get a heartwarming feeling as the two lovers fawn over each other. It reminds me when I first met Bob, and it's always great to recall that.

"Bobbie, I'm having a small party at my house Saturday night and I'd love it if you and Bob can make it. Please bring your wonderful governess I've met along with her husband. Bring little Tilly as well."

"I'll check with Bob, but I'm sure he'd love to be there. I've read about your house in *Architectural Digest* and I'm dying to see it. What's the occasion, if I may ask?"

"It's Rick's idea and it's a surprise. Hope to see you Saturday."

At 7:30 on Saturday we pulled into the long driveway leading to Jenny Bateman's house. It's a beautiful waterfront mansion on Champlin Creek in East Islip. From what I've read about the house, it was built in 1929 on 3.2 acres. The architect was famous for his understated elegance. An Olympic sized swimming pool graced the sloping lawn leading to the creek. A valet parker opened the door for us, and a butler led us down a hallway to the ballroom. Jenny had said it would be a small party, but I estimated that 250 people were there, including a large contingent from Robot Depot. Jenny had told me that she had thoughts about selling the house after the death of her husband Mike, but she had grown to love the place, so she never got around to putting it on the market.

The "small party" was one of the most opulent events I'd ever attended. Jenny is accustomed to doing things in a big way.

A governess in an evening gown escorted little Tilly to a large room on the opposite side of the house where other young children played, entertained by a steady cast of amusing character actors.

Jane grabbed me by the arm and said, "Holy shit, I thought your house in East Hampton was fabulous, Bob, but this place competes with it."

"Billions of dollars go a long way," I said. "Jenny has just made the Forbes 400 List of wealthiest Americans for the fifth year in a row, with a net worth of 12 billion, placing her at position number 38. Jenny isn't afraid to spend money, and she has it to spend."

A string quartet played classical music in the sunroom next to the ballroom. Classy, as I would expect of Jenny Bateman. At 8:30 p.m., the string quartet moved from the sunroom into the ballroom. My gut told me that something big was about to happen. As the quartet played a gentle classical piece, Rick walked to the middle of the ballroom holding hands with Jenny, smiling at her. Jenny, who is a beautiful woman by any objective standard, looked heavenly in her gorgeous light blue dress. And Rick, wearing a tuxedo, looked like he belonged on the cover of *GQ*.

"Oh my God, Bob, I think I know what's about to happen." My romantic heart was fluttering wildly. But what was about to happen was a surprise, especially to me.

"Ladies and gentlemen, I propose a toast to a wonderful lady and a dear friend, the person who is responsible for us being here tonight. Please raise your glasses to Bobbie Nelson. Jenny and I know her as Yenta, the matchmaker."

I lost it, I totally fucking lost it, embarrassing myself with sobs, happy sobs.

Rick then knelt on one knee in front of Jenny and grabbed her left hand. Oh my God, can this really be happening?

"Jenny Bateman," he said as he slipped a ring on her finger, "I've concluded how long I want to be with you—Forever. Please be my wife."

He stood and they kissed.

"Forever it is, Rick. I accept your proposal. I love you," Jenny said with considerable volume in her sweet voice.

The assembled guests went absolutely batshit. I think of myself as a cop, a *tough* cop. So, what are these friggin tears all about? They're tears for a good friend, a dear friend, for two people who so obviously love each other. Whatever role I played in bringing these two together is right up there with the greatest things I've ever accomplished, second only to marrying Bob and adopting Tilly.

Jane was doing an excellent job of supplying me with a fresh supply of tissues to wipe my tears away. I think maybe I'll officially change my middle name to Yenta.

"I think of you as a dear friend, Bobbie," Jane said. "Tonight, I realize that you're not just a great friend but a great woman for bringing those two together."

I hugged Jane, grabbing more tissues from her hand as I did.

Bob walked up next to me and put his arm around my waist, gently brushing his hand by my ass as he did so. We've been married over two years, and you'd think I'd get used to that gesture. Never happened. I felt a fire ignite inside me. I stared into his gorgeous hazel eyes.

"You know who they remind me of, honey?"

"Us."

I'd been embarrassing myself with my constant flowing tears, so I figured I'd embarrass myself a little more with a public display of affection for the man of my life. I wrapped my arms around Bob's neck and kissed him with probably more passion than was appropriate for the setting.

"You know where I want you to take me later, Bob?"

"To the mountaintop?" (our codeword for a mind-blowing orgasm).

"Oh, yes, to the tippy top of the mountain. And you'll be there with me."

I briefly considered asking Bob to take me to the car and screw my brains out in the back seat, but I figured I'd try for a little decorum. Fortunately, there's no such thing as decorum in our bedroom. Later can't come soon enough.

What a fabulous evening. We watched our two good friends become engaged, something I had played a part in, I'm happy to say. And the evening became even better as Bob and I got horny as hell.

But then an annoying thought crossed my mind. We're at war.

And the war is far from over, as I'd soon discover.

CHAPTER 34

Peter Solomon walked into his private office for his meeting with his aide, Gloria Wetherill. Gloria had told him she had something important to talk about.

Gloria sat on the chair in front of his desk, her legs curled under her. She was naked.

Solomon stifled a laugh as he realized that Gloria was getting increasingly aggressive in trying to control him, to try to wrap him around her finger. Little did she know that he had her wrapped around *his* finger. But, although he knew exactly what she was trying to do, her hot naked body told him that the meeting could begin with a little pleasant diversion.

He walked over to Gloria's chair and stood in front of her. She reached up and unbuckled his pants and lowered them to the floor. He was eagerly awaiting her, a fact made obvious by his stiff erection. She looked up into his eyes as she took him in her mouth. She slowly worked her magic, having done quite a bit of research on Internet porn sites to make sure she had just the right moves. He grabbed her hands and pulled her to a standing position. Then he sat down and pulled her on top of him. He was pleased to feel that she was quite wet with readiness, and he wouldn't need to waste a lot of time with foreplay to get her started. He inserted himself into her. She gasped and squealed as she had practiced. "Oh, shit, Oh, fuck," she yelled. She had noticed recently that the chairman seemed to be aroused when she used foul words during sex. And what he found arousing, Gloria would provide.

"I'm coming soon, Gloria."

She could feel him about to climax and she pretended to do so at the same time, faking an orgasm that she thought was worthy of an Oscar. She screamed, writhing under him, matching his thrusts as she glanced at her watch. She always kept careful track of time and didn't want their upcoming meeting to be delayed much longer. Carefully stifling a yawn, she looked at him with dreamy eyes and said, "Mr. Chairman, that was simply wonderful."

"It's time for our meeting," Solomon said as he lifted her off his lap. She was amazed at how he could go from passion to business in a wink of an eye. But then she wasn't feeling passionate at all, although you would never notice from her well-rehearsed sexual performance. She did not look at Peter Solomon with passion; she looked at him as a project.

They went to the bathroom to freshen up and got dressed. She wore a form hugging blouse that showed an eye-filling view of her breasts, thinking it a good idea to let him know that there was more action to come—if he wanted it, of course.

"So, Gloria, you said that you had some important matters to discuss. Let me hear it."

"It concerns the Re-Education Project, Mr. Chairman, specifically our use of Ambien to make the subjects amenable to hypnotism."

"Our use of Ambien is strictly top secret are you aware?"

"Of course, sir, but I think we may have a problem. One that needs a solution. One of our spies believes that the Americans have discovered an antidote to the drug, one that can completely reverse the re-education. It can be administered after the re-education has been completed, and it can totally reverse the hypnosis. This could change all our plans completely."

"Contact the head of our security department and tell him to come here immediately. But change your blouse first. That view is for my eyes only."

CHAPTER 35

Bobbie

Having decided that they'd put things off long enough, Jenny Bateman and Rick Patton decided to marry just one month after their impromptu engagement party. At Rick's urging, Jenny decided to keep her maiden name because she had become quite famous in the business and investment communities as head of the world's largest automation company. I thought it was a good idea, especially since I kept my maiden name, Nelson, after we married. Bob was also well-known, although in different circles. For us, it was mainly about a book deal and marketing. We may have different last names, but we think of ourselves as one person.

The wedding was held at the beautiful Bourne Mansion, once a Vanderbilt Estate, in Oakdale, Long Island. I recalled reading that was the place where Fred Astaire met his wife, Phyllis Livingston Potter.

We were blown away when Rick asked Bob to be his best man and Jenny asked me to be her maid of honor. They are definitely our good friends, especially since I was responsible for rekindling their relationship.

Given Jenny's money and the size of Robot Depot, the wedding could have been a huge elaborate affair, but only 300 guests attended. The wedding ceremony was held at St. Mark's Episcopal Church in Islip. Father Rick Sampson, our old friend, presided. Jenny had asked us for a recommendation. I think they see Bob and me as good luck charms after our matchmaking dinner party a few months ago. Luxury tour buses would take those who wanted a ride to Oakdale for the reception.

Because he was on active duty with the Marines, thanks to General Mike, Bob wore his dress uniform instead of a tuxedo. The carefully tailored uniform embraced Bob's beautiful muscular body. He looked so goddam handsome I wished I could hide him from all the women who kept staring at him.

As we expected, the wedding reception was a beautiful and classy affair.

After Father Rick pronounced them man and wife, it was touching to watch them kiss and hug, two people who obviously loved each other deeply. Bob, God bless him, kept me fed with a constant supply of tissues.

Unlike the engagement party, the wedding reception included an 18-piece band that knew how to play rock & roll. I remembered our own wedding, and the first time I realized that Bob is a fabulous dancer. I'm pretty good myself, I must admit. We spun around the dance floor doing the Lindy and I was embarrassed to see a large group of people surround us and clap as we danced.

It was a great evening, a nice break from the goddam war we're involved in.

And no doubt about it, as Captain Bob reminds me, we are at war.

CHAPTER 36

Bob

B
obbie and I decided to continue our ongoing tour of Long Island to see if we could find any clues that may help to stop the quarantine. We were near the Brooklyn Navy Yard, so we decided to have lunch in the Officer's Club, gaining admission because of Bob's status as an active duty Marine captain, although he wore civilian clothing on this trip.

We were led to a table by the window, and who was sitting at the next table but Admiral Ashley Patterson and her husband, Commander Jack Thurber. We had become friends with Ashley and Jack a couple of years ago when we investigated a case that involved the Navy. It suddenly occurred to Bobbie and me that our recent time travel adventures made our meeting with Ashley and Jack a fortunate coincidence.

Ashley became world famous a few years ago when she was a captain and commanded a nuclear guided missile cruiser, the *USS California*. The reason for her fame is that the *California* encountered a wormhole near Charleston, South Carolina as it cruised to Fort

Sumter for a reenactment of the start of the Civil War, which began with the confederate bombardment of the fort. Bobbie and I are no longer time travel sceptics, and we found the story fascinating. After cruising through the wormhole, the ship found itself in the year 1861 on April 10, two days before the beginning of the war.

Although I doubted it at the time—I no longer do—Ashley ordered the ship to head north to meet with Gideon Welles, who was then Secretary of the Navy, and with President Abraham Lincoln. At Lincoln's urging, on his command actually, the *California* became part of the Union forces.

Ashley and her crew, which included a handsome junior officer, Lieutenant Jack Thurber, changed history by engaging the Confederacy at the Battle of Bull Run. The history books listed the battle as a Confederate victory, but Ashley and company changed that, aided by the *California's* Tomahawk missiles. That, and other battles, shortened the terrible war and ensured a quick Union victory. The Confederates called the *California, The Gray Ship.* Ashley and Jack fell in love and married shortly after the *California* returned to the year 2013. You can't make this shit up, not if you're a time traveler. Jack, a famous author and journalist, wrote a book with Ashley as co-author. The title, appropriately enough, was *The Gray Ship.* It became an international best seller and revised a lot of people's thinking about the phenomenon of time travel. It took a trip to Camp Hero to convince Bobbie and me that time travel was for real. Hell, we did it so how can we doubt it?

Ashley Patterson is a tall, stunningly beautiful African American woman with a gifted speaking voice. Jack was never bothered about playing second fiddle to his lovely wife. He kept himself busy as a highly paid consultant with major newspapers and cranking out best-selling books regularly.

When we walked over to their table, Ashley and Jack stood to greet us. Classy people.

Ashley's most recent job, I had read, was Commandant of the United States Naval Academy, which is also her alma mater. I asked her what she was doing in the Brooklyn Navy Yard, a long haul from Annapolis.

"Jack and I were here for a commissioning ceremony for the new base commander. I don't have to tell you why we're still here. I guess that's why you two Manhattanites are here too—the Long Island quarantine. Actually, I'm no longer Commandant of the Naval Academy. I have a new assignment, one with lots of action I'm pleased to say. I'm now the Commanding Officer of Carrier Strike Group 2123. It consists of two frigates, a destroyer, and of course, a carrier. The *USS Gerald R. Ford* is my flagship. This handsome commander here is my Chief of Staff, although I still help with the dishes."

I had forgotten Ashly's nonstop sense of humor. Also, from my previous encounters with them, I recalled that Ashley and Jack are a close, loving couple. They remind me of Bobbie and me.

"Ashley, Jack, what's your take on this bizarre quarantine we're under?" Bobbie said.

"It's frustrating as hell," Ashley said. "I have enough firepower under my command to take out a small country, but as of now we're stuck because we can't do much to fight a quarantine."

"Don't ask me why I think this," I said, "but something tells me your strike group will be quite busy before long."

CHAPTER 37

Bobbie

W e've got a problem." Bennie Weinberg said. Our committee, which General Mike Bennet named "The Un-Education Committee," met at Suffolk County Police headquarters in a conference room next to Mike's office. Un-Education Committee is a dumb name, I thought, but then I realized that it does capture exactly what we're up to, reversing the effects of the re-education hypnosis of the Committee of Freedom. Besides Bob and me, the other committee members present were Commissioner Mike Townsend, Bennie and Maggie Weinberg, and of course, General Mike. Jenny Bateman, and her new husband Rick Patton were also committee members but couldn't attend this meeting as they were on their long-delayed honeymoon. It had snowed like a bitch the night before, being late February, leaving six inches on the ground. It took forever to get to Yaphank from our house in East Hampton. Bob requested that Commissioner Mike assign us a four-wheel drive SUV, and Mike immediately agreed. Mike takes good care of his BBs. After the meeting we would pick up a Toyota Land Cruiser for our trek back east.

I sat at the conference table, but I was uncomfortable as hell. I was eight months pregnant and the baby was due in three weeks, Mid-March. I wore a pair of Uggs, not just to protect my feet from the cold, but also to cover up the compression stockings on my swollen ankles. This baby can't come soon enough.

"So, what's the problem, Bennie?" General Mike asked, his fingers tented.

"The problem is a big one, General. We've noticed that a significant number of people who have gone through the re-education program are not responding to treatments with Torlazine. As you ordered, we keep careful statistics on the number of people treated with Torlazine, and it seems to have no effect on a startling number of newer people. They remain Committee of Freedom zombies. We thought we had the perfect antidote to the problem, but an increasing number of people appear to be immune to Torlazine."

"Is the drug working on anybody?" General Mike asked.

"Yes, quite a few, but it seems that at some point in the past couple of months only those who were subjected to Ambien are able to be cured. Bottom line, they've begun using a different drug in their hypnosis program, one that isn't affected by Torlazine. Fortunately, it's a recent development, meaning that the vast number of re-educated zombies can still be cured."

"How is the identification program going?" I asked. "Are we still able to identify those who have gone through the re-education from their manner of speech?"

"That's an equally big problem, Bobbie," Bennie said. "Until recently we've been able to identify the 're-educated' by the way they talked including the code speech they learned. When we hear 'Our leader and savior,' or the New World Order,' we would lock onto that person as a target for Torlazine. No longer that easy. The latest group of 're-educated' people speak normally, making it difficult to impossible to identify them."

Bennie, who usually keeps his emotions to himself, seemed upset.

"It's been six goddam months since this Long Island quarantine started, and now we find that we're back to square one," Bennie said.

"Ok, folks, we're going to change our strategy 180 degrees," General Mike said. "We have no choice."

Nobody has ever accused General Mike of thinking or acting slowly. He's used to making command decisions.

"And what will be the new strategy, if you don't mind me asking, sir?" I said.

"Military force."

CHAPTER 38

Bob

Bobbie is almost nine months pregnant, and she'll soon go into labor. It's March 12, and, thank goodness, the snow has melted and the temperature moderated. I've carefully planned our drive to Southampton Hospital when Bobbie is due, a 30-minute trip. Jane and Steve look after Bobbie almost as carefully as I do, and we've rehearsed exactly what we'd do when she goes into labor. Those two are so much like family, I'd love to adopt them as brother and sister.

Tilly had gone to bed and was soundly asleep after an afternoon of playing with Lucky. The four of us decided to watch the political convention of the Committee of Freedom, as upsetting as the idea seemed. Ignoring the Committee of Freedom was a tempting idea, given how it upsets us, but Bobbie and I know that our job is to stay on top of these creeps and follow their every move. We sat around the den in front of the TV as Jane served snacks. Bobbie munched on a stick of celery, even as she lovingly eyed the broiled chicken with mac-and-cheese casserole that Jane had put out.

"Hey, hon, what will you snack on after you give birth?"

"Two pepperoni pizzas and a case of beer."

She grabbed another stick of celery.

"Why would they have a political convention in mid-March in the Northeast when the weather is anything but predictable?" Jane said.

"It's typical of those bastards," I said. "They hope the weather will be bad to cut down on demonstrations and ensure that the majority of those present are their people. And it seems to be working. We may be having a mild spell here on Long Island, but Boston, where the convention is held, is under a winter storm alert with snow and sleet expected."

At 8 p.m. the convention began.

"Good evening, ladies and gentlemen, Brett Baier reporting for *Fox News*, bringing you live coverage of the first nominating convention of the controversial Committee of Freedom Party in Boston, Massachusetts. Winter is reminding us of its presence here in Boston, with snow and sleet predicted. As we've been announcing for the past several weeks, it appears likely that there will be only one candidate put forth, none other than Committee of Freedom Chairman, Peter Solomon. We don't yet know who his running mate will be, but I expect to be announcing that shortly.

"As we've been reporting for months, The Committee of Freedom is surrounded by controversy. What I just said is a vast understatement. It's conventional wisdom, if not common knowledge, that the infamous quarantine of Long Island is the doing of this party and its Chairman, Peter Solomon, although Solomon denies it.

"The party's administrative director, Dwayne Peterson, is

approaching the microphone. He just said that he was proud and happy to announce Peter Solomon's running mate, Colonel Jake Stratton, US Army, retired."

Colonel Stratton walked up to the microphone.

"I couldn't be happier to be the vice-presidential candidate and running mate of our leader and savior, Chairman Peter Solomon, the man who will lead us into the New World Order."

"Holy shit," the four of us said.

"Our leader and savior? It looks like Solomon's running mate is a Re-Educated Robot from Montauk," I said. "Maybe they'll wear armbands and come up with an arms-out salute."

"And he's a retired senior military officer," Bobbie said, looking as if she were about to throw up.

The two of them did the traditional walk around the platform with their hands raised and waving, a normal sight at any political convention. But there was a difference. Neither man was married, so they were not accompanied by wives. I did notice that Peter Solomon waved to a foxy chick in a low-cut red dress sensuously draped over her *let's-party body*.

"Ladies and gentlemen," Director Peterson said, "It is my pleasure and honor to introduce the next President of the United States, our leader and savior, Chairman Peter Solomon."

As if on cue, the Committee of Freedom robots chanted, "So-lo-mon, So-lo-mon, So-lo-mon." That went on for 10 minutes.

He walked around the platform waving and raising his joined hands to the air. He wore a smile, but I thought it looked more like a wicked grin.

"My friends and colleagues," he began in a deep resonant voice, "for too long our nation has been under the yolk of outdated thoughts and ideas, ideas that bring us nothing but pessimism and despair, drowning us in old ways of thinking. We have been trained to think as we have been programmed to think, not with our own minds but someone else's. I'm happy to say that those times are over. It is my honor and privilege to introduce you to a new world, a world of exciting hopefulness. Soon, the days of walking in lockstep with the crowd will be over. Gone will be the days of blind obedience to idiotic thinking. My friends, we are about to embark on the New World Order."

"Our leader and savior - our leader and savior - our leader and savior," chanted the robots for the next five minutes as confetti floated down from the ceiling.

Lucky the bulldog growled, ran up to the TV, raised his leg, and urinated on the cabinet.

"So, there you have it, ladies and gentlemen," Bret Baier said from his broadcast booth. "A political platform that is amazingly short on specifics, but long on crowd-pleasing platitudes. We're still waiting to see who the Democrats or Republicans will pick to oppose him, but whoever they are will need a lot of energy to counter the enthusiasm of this crowd. This is Bret Baier, signing off for *Fox News*."

I looked at Bobbie, hoping that she wouldn't have an evening bout of morning sickness after the crap we just watched.

"Okay, guys," I said, "I suggest we do a little unscientific polling after what we all just saw. Lucky has already voted with his hind leg. I'd like to hear everybody's honest opinion of Solomon's performance. Try to keep your personal feelings out of it, and just say what you felt as you watched and listened to him. Jane, you go first."

"Impressive as hell," Jane said. "I have no idea what he was talking about because he didn't say anything specific, but he got to my heart with his powerful words. It was stirring."

"Steve?"

"I agree with Jane. I found the guy extremely impressive, even though I needed to put my brain on hold as I listened to him. I found him moving, I'm ashamed to say. That man knows how to grab people's emotions and sway a crowd."

"Bobbie?"

"I'm embarrassed to say this, but I too was moved by his words, even though they had no substance whatsoever. That man is one of the finest public speakers I've ever heard. He had my heart thumping."

Bobbie, with an undergraduate degree from Yale and a law degree from the University of Chicago, is one of the smartest people I've ever met. And this scumbag even impressed her.

"Okay, my turn. I agree with everything you guys said. That son of a bitch had me in the palm of his hand, although for the life of me I don't know why. I think, as you folks said, it was his impressive and powerful delivery. So, this creep, who we all despise, managed to move each of us emotionally with his words. If this bastard manages to pull off the next election, I think we'll be looking at America's first dictator."

I almost regretted our little straw poll—because it scared the hell out of me. Could the American people elect this totalitarian piece of shit? Time will tell.

CHAPTER 39

The *USS Gerald R. Ford*, America's newest and largest aircraft carrier, steamed in the Atlantic Ocean with Long Island off its starboard side. It was also Admiral Ashley Patterson's flagship, the lead vessel for Carrier Strike Group 2123. General Mike Bennet, in consultation with the White House and the Secretaries of Defense and Navy, determined that military force was necessary to end the quarantine of Long Island. Dr. Benjamin Weinberg's brilliant idea to neutralize the hypnotic grip on people fell short because the enemy was using a new substance that was impervious to the curative effects of the drug Torlazine. The thinking, at the top echelons of the military, was 'once a robot always a robot.' It was now up to traditional military intervention.

Admiral Patterson stood on the flag bridge of the *Ford* next to her husband and Chief of Staff, Jack Thurber. In an article in the *Navy Times*, the reporter stated that Admiral Patterson and Commander Thurber are not only two of the most powerful military officers in the service, but they seem to never want to leave each other's sides.

Admiral Patterson called Commander Dwight Baxter, the Air Operations Officer, and ordered the strike.

Although a determined Marine officer for many years, General

Bennet admitted to himself that he was nervous, extremely nervous. The reason for his concern was that the latest wave of "re-educated" people did not show the symptoms of having undergone hypnosis as in the past. Until recently it was easy to spot people who had gone through the re-education just by listening to what they had do say. If the person referred to our "leader and savior" or the New World Order, you knew you were dealing with a re-educated zombie. So, the problem was how to determine if a person was re-educated or not. If a person had gone through re-education, could he or she be trusted in a combat setting? He recalled the military genius, Carl von Clausewitz writing about the "fog of war," and how he said that, "No operational plan can, with any degree of safety, go further than the first encounter with the enemy." And what if you're not certain just who the enemy is? Bennet popped a Maalox, something he usually prides himself on avoiding.

———————

The *Ford* had just entered New York Harbor when it launched a squadron of 24 F/A 18 Super Hornets. Their targets were a tank and infantry brigade nestled under the Whitestone Bridge in Queens. As the 24 jets approached the Whitestone Bridge, suddenly 10 of them left formation and climbed sharply. Commander Dwight Baxter, the Air Ops commander, shouted into his radio, ordering the straying jets to regroup. The ten jets dove and aimed for the remaining aircraft in the flight, opening fire with cannons and air-to-air missiles. None of the pilots in the remaining planes were expecting the attack, and all 14 planes were destroyed and their pilots killed. The 10 attacking planes, piloted by re-educated officers, flew to a secret base in New Jersey that was controlled by the Committee of Freedom.

Never in his long career in the Marines had General Bennet commanded an operation that was a such a complete failure.

CHAPTER 40

Bob

As the second in command of the "Un-Education Committee" I convened a meeting at Jenny Bateman's office at Robot Depot. I enjoy watching Jenny and Rick joke around and stare at each other. Bobbie did a great job of bringing these two together. It lightened the mood at this stressful meeting.

Bennie and Maggie Weinberg showed up a few minutes later, followed by SCPD Commissioner Mike Townsend and General Mike Bennet.

General Mike looked like hell, I couldn't help but notice. He normally has the vitality of the Energizer Bunny, but he looked somehow crushed. His normal smiling face was covered in a frown.

"I'm sure you haven't heard about it because it was absolutely top secret, but my planned military operation was an utter failure," General Mike said.

I don't believe I'd ever heard General Mike use the words "operation" and "failure" in the same sentence. He told us about the debacle of an air strike launched from the aircraft carrier *USS Gerald R. Ford*. No, we hadn't heard about it because it was, indeed, top secret, and none of us had the precious "need to know" even though we all had top-secret clearances.

"I can't believe that I haven't been relieved of duty or demoted," Mike said. "Fourteen pilots were killed and a few billion dollars of defense budget money went up in smoke. President Fenton called me this morning to ask me to continue on as Commandant of the Marine Corps. I'm amazed that he still has such faith in me. So, let me tell you what happened. In the 24 planes in the attack squadron targeting the tanks and artillery under the Whitestone Bridge, apparently 10 of the pilots were on the other side and opened fire on the 14 other aircraft, destroying them all. You heard me—10 pilots were on the *other side*, and none of us had a hint. I interviewed the flight commander on the *Ford*, and he told me that none of the traitors showed any strange behavior or language. I also spoke to Admiral Ashley Patterson, the finest admiral in the Navy in my opinion. She confirmed what the Air Boss said, that there were no indications that any crewmember had gone through re-education. There was no talking about 'our leader and savior,' and nothing about the 'New World Order.' Because none of them raised any suspicions, they all flew below our radar, to make a bad pun."

"General Mike, if I may," I said, "I think it's inappropriate for you to blame yourself. I think it's obvious, to me anyway, that we're in a war that we're not accustomed to. How do you kill the enemy if you don't know who he is? We've got a lot of adjusting to do."

"Any thoughts, Bennie?" the general said.

"Well, even though my mother hates it, I'm known as Bennie the Bullshit Detector. Yes, I'll admit that I'm good at detecting lies."

"You're the best, honey," Maggie said, smiling at him.

"Well, thanks, baby, but I'm here to tell you that I can't possibly interrogate every fucking member of the armed forces, not to mention government officials…"

"Or business executives," Jenny chimed in.

"It can take me an afternoon of listening to testimony before I can give an expert opinion that the witness is lying. Sure, if a guy spouts bullshit about our 'leader and savior,' or the 'New World Order,' you don't need me to tell you the guy's a flake. You can figure it out yourself. But we're in a new era of Committee of Freedom hypnosis. It's hard to spot a 're-educated' person if he doesn't talk weird. That makes it scary as hell for a military operation if you don't know if the guy next to you is friend or foe. General, I thought your idea of military intervention was great, although my military experience was limited to service as a combat surgeon."

"A highly decorated combat surgeon," Maggie added. She's really proud of her Bennie.

"Folks, we have enough mental power in this room to run a small city," General Mike said. "Anybody have any thoughts?"

"Drones," Jenny said.

We all stared at her.

"It takes very few desk pilots to control a flight of drones, not to mention automatic drones operated by GPS. Because there are so few people at the controls they can be carefully observed and monitored."

"But, Jenny," I said. "Aren't the pilotless aircraft you manufacture those small helicopter drones. They can be deadly, God knows, but can they be used effectively in a military operation?"

"If what I'm about to say leaves this room I'm risking prison time, but let me tell you about a huge new contract we have with the Department of Defense. Robot Depot has been selected to replace the older Predator drones. Frankly, the new models we make are far superior to the Predators, which, as you know, are sizeable fully equipped combat aircraft armed with air-to-air and air-to-surface missiles. It has a 66-foot wingspan and a payload of 3,800 pounds. It can carry a variety of weapons, including Hellfire missiles and 500-pound laser-guided bombs. It has a range of 1,000 nautical miles and can operate as high as 50,000 feet. And we don't need to worry about a drone going through 're-education.' They could be the answer. If I may offer some targeting recommendations, I think we should destroy those goddam Re-Education auditoriums in Montauk."

Rick, Jenny's new husband, walked around the table, took her in his arms and kissed her.

"Does my old lady know how to kick ass or not?" Rick yelled.

"Call me an old lady once more and I'll show you some ass kicking," Jenny said, laughing.

"Jenny, you're brilliant," General Mike said. "This could be the answer we're looking for. Do you have any military experience, Jenny?"

"I was once a carrier-based fighter pilot in the Navy. I used to fly F/A 18s like the ones you recently lost, General."

I was stunned. "Jenny, you never told us you were a fighter pilot," I said, as Bobbie slapped the table, her eyes wide as frisbees. Holy shit, our sweet, gentle friend is a trained fighter pilot, an aerial warrior.

"It never came up in polite conversation, Bob. My maiden name, my Navy name, was Jennifer Brandon, Lieutenant Jennifer Brandon. You folks can rest assured that when it comes to aerial combat, I know my shit."

Her husband Rick sat there, beaming.

"Jenny, are these new drones operational and what are they called?"

"Yes, General, they're fully operational. We call them *Gates*, short for *Gates of Hell*. Give me the word, General and I'll order production to be ramped up."

"Jenny, you are one great American," the general said. "Yes, please ramp up production."

"I have now given you folks enough top-secret information to send me to prison for life. Please keep your lips zipped. I will call my contacts at the Department of Defense and let them know you'll be calling, General. Please cover my ass by telling them I was acting under your orders, which is true enough. They like to coordinate operations."

"How many drones do you have right now that are ready for delivery?"

"We have 50 *Gates*, 200 smaller fixed-wing aircraft and hundreds of helicopter drones. All of them can be armed with missiles and bombs. It's not my position to say this, General, but how about we end this fucking Long Island quarantine tomorrow, the day after at the latest, so as to give us enough time to arm the drones?"

The end of the quarantine—Yesss!

CHAPTER 41

Bob

General Bennet likes to take command of operations himself, but he realized that he needed a lot of technical assistance for the drone attack on the Long Island quarantine. There would be three areas of operation, and the attacks would take place simultaneously. The tank and infantry brigades guarding the Whitestone Bridge were the first targets, then followed by drone attacks on the 25 gunboats patrolling the shores of Long Island. After the Whitestone Bridge attacks there would be attacks on the smaller battle tank units stationed at the other bridges and tunnels leading to Long Island. The final part of the plan would be to destroy the buildings that house the Re-Education Project auditoriums in Montauk, including the one that had just been erected a month ago. Jenny Bateman, with her newly disclosed knowledge of aerial warfare, would be a key. Also, she is an expert on drone aircraft, her company being the largest manufacturer of them. General Bennet, a widower, told Jenny that if she hadn't recently married, he would propose to her. Also, she is an obvious expert on drone aircraft

As General Mike's newly announced chief of staff, I would have my hands full. Thank God Bobbie is at my side. The idea of handling any major project, whether a criminal investigation, or in this case a military operation, without Bobbie, simply does not fit into my thinking. Bobbie's not part of my life, she *is* my life.

Launching a major aerial attack from a corporate office made my stomach quiver. But, with Jenny Bateman's military knowledge and the world class communications of Robot Depot, I agreed that it was the best place to base our operations. My job was to coordinate communications between our location and the office of General Dwight Thompson, Chairman of the Joint Chiefs of Staff in Washington.

Jenny ordered five *Gates* (Gates of Hell), the larger drones that are replacing the Predators, to attack the tank and infantry brigades under the Whitestone Bridge. The attack would consist of air-to-surface missiles, small cannon fire, and 500-pound laser-guided bombs. The missiles and cannon shells were tipped with armor piercing steel. Another drone flew above the formation, relaying real-time video coverage of the attack below.

We sat around the table in the main conference room. The lights were dim to give the drone operators a clear view of their screens. General Mike was at the head of the table, his laptop poised in front of him. To his right was Jenny Bateman, and next to her were two of her most trusted engineers, and four drone pilots, who operated their pilotless flying robots from the computer screens in front of them. It was a bizarre scene. I had a hard time believing that we were about to launch a gigantic military operation from a corporate boardroom.

Bobbie sat next to me, occasionally squeezing my hand for support.

I've been in combat before and I recognized the feelings in the pit of my stomach. Sure, we were launching an air strike with pilotless drones, but I was a wreck because so much depended on the success

180

of this operation. Although I tried to keep it from everybody, I was scared shitless.

It all happened blindingly fast. Within five minutes, every tank in view was in flames, some of them blown to thousands of pieces by the armor piercing missiles. This was war, and General Mike felt he had no choice but to attack the infantry with deadly force as well. Some of the drones dropped bombs laden with Torlazine, but, because we couldn't count on the targets having taken Ambien, General Mike ordered lethal strikes with traditional weapons. After they fired their missiles, the drones dropped 500-pound laser-guided bombs on the infantry units. The drones then flew to the Bronx side of the bridge and attacked the smaller tank units stationed there. We watched the same destruction that we saw on the Whitestone side of the bridge, the view provided by the surveillance drone flying above the chaos. On the Bronx side there was some resistance, the units having been alerted by the attack on the Whitestone side. We lost one Gates of Hell drone, and five smaller ones.

Standard military doctrine holds that an aerial attack has to be followed up with ground infantry. But this was a war like no other, and our limited goal was to break the Long Island quarantine, so we relied primarily on aerial assault. However, 50 Bradley Fighting vehicles and 200 Humvees were dispatched from Fort Dix in New Jersey. As soon as the tank and infantry brigades on either side of the Whitestone Bridge were destroyed, the Bradleys and Humvees, with a battalion of soldiers aboard, stormed across the bridge toward Long Island to secure it.

After dropping or firing all of their ordnance, the drones returned to their airfield where they were re-armed for their next attack.

The two buildings in Montauk that held the Re-Education Project auditoriums, including the new one, required heavy firepower. Six Tomahawk cruise missiles were launched from the *USS Gerald R. Ford*, Admiral Patterson's flagship, steaming off Eastern Long

Island. Because the first military strike, which saw 10 pilots switch sides, Admiral Patterson ordered each of the two Tomahawk batteries to be commanded by four senior officers, who would carefully monitor the missile technicians. A Tomahawk missile is 18 feet in length, 20 inches in diameter and weighs 2,900 pounds. It's armed with 1,000 pounds of high explosives. Our video feedback showed us that both buildings engulfed in flames and explosions. The surveillance drone flew far above the buildings. BDA (Battle Damage Assessment) confirmed that both buildings were totally destroyed. The meeting was interrupted with shouts and applause. There would be no more zombie graduates of the Re-Education Project. We saw Ashley Patterson's face on the screens. "Targets have been destroyed," she said calmly. She is one class act.

The 25 gunboats steaming off Long Island were attacked with electronically guided torpedoes by five submarines that had been dispatched to the area, aided by hundreds of armed helicopter drones. Within minutes, all the gunboats were destroyed.

The various battles continued for a total of 45 minutes, which I found amazing. This was a war of technology, very high technology.

The war against the Committee of Freedom was far from over, but the Long Island quarantine was ended. Ingress and egress from the island was now open, including air travel in and out. General Mike flew to Washington where he would assume his duties as Commandant of the Marine Corps at the Pentagon.

It was time to get back to normal. But what *is* normal?

CHAPTER 42

Bobbie

It never felt better to drive through the Queens-Midtown tunnel on our way to our apartment on Park Row in Manhattan. Jane and Steve will close title shortly on their condo right near ours. They had signed a contract just before the Long Island quarantine.

It was great to be back in New York City, even though we love our place in East Hampton. At least here in Manhattan, our neighbor won't be walking around in her tiny bikini, a little yellow number that accentuates her pert little ass and her full tits. And more importantly, Bob won't be staring at her hot body all the time. I'm due to deliver the baby within the next two weeks, and I was beginning to feel like an elephant, a very grouchy elephant.

Can it just be a hormonal thing that I notice Bob staring at our foxy neighbor all the time? I even get bothered as hell when he looks at Jane, who wears a bikini beautifully. I'm pretty self-confident, and I know that when not pregnant I'm not hard to look at, but it was driving me nuts to see Bob looking at a sexy body, a body that doesn't belong to me.

Okay, time to grow up.

"Jane should be here shortly, honey." Bob said.

"Why does Jane need to be here? You and I are home to take care of Tilly, why do we need somebody else?"

"Jane wants to be here to help, honey. You're due to go into labor at any time."

"Jane wants to be here, or do *you* want her to be here?"

"Hey, what's up, baby? Jane is always here when we need help."

"I hope she won't be wearing a bikini," I said, wishing I could recapture the words before they left my mouth.

Bob laughed, walked over and hugged me. I think he just realized that he's married to a born-again asshole. I grabbed his collar, pulled him in and kissed him, a deep, hot, take-me-right-now-on-the-kitchen-table kind of kiss.

"I get your feeling, honey, do I ever. God knows we've had plenty of sex during your pregnancy, but we're now at the eleventh hour I think maybe we should hold off a bit. You're having a tough time even sitting."

"Who said that I want to sit?"

"Hey, hot mama, let's slow down. Jane should be here any minute."

Oh shit, Jane. I can't wait. If she's wearing anything tight fitting, I think I'll loan her a caftan or a mumu.

At 6:30, Jane walked in, wearing a pair of baggy jeans and an oversized NYU sweatshirt. She's such a sweetheart and I love her like a sister. I just wish I could get over this crazy jealousy I'm feeling over any good-looking woman within eye-view of Bob.

Nothing like hormones to make the heart grow weirder. Steve, who had an early morning appointment, was staying at their place in Westchester. Jane will be staying at our apartment tonight in the room we've given her. Our apartment is huge, at 3,000 square feet, and had four full bedroom suites, one of which we've assigned to Jane. When she goes to bed I think I'll put a piece of tape over her door to make sure it isn't opened during the night. Holy shit, where the hell is my brain going?

After Tilly went to sleep. Bob, Jane and I watched TV to catch up on the latest moves of the weird Committee of Freedom. At least the goddam Long Island quarantine is over. Peter Solomon vigorously denies the Committee had anything to do with it, despite a mounting body of evidence that it was Solomon's idea and that the Committee pulled it off. The screen suddenly filled with that disgusting face of his. We're definitely not done with this piece of shit.

"Remember our little straw poll we held in East Hampton when we watched Solomon at his convention?" Bob said. "All four of us agreed that the guy is a mesmerizing public speaker and has an uncanny way of pulling people to his point of view? Something tells me that bastard is going to be part of our future."

"Hey, Bob, don't give me morning sickness at this hour of the night."

———————

I woke up at 5:30 a.m. with a wicked contraction. I was tired as hell and ignored it. Then, 10 minutes later came another one. I shook Bob by the shoulder.

"I think it's time, honey. We should get to the hospital."

"Jane, it's time," Bob yelled as he pounded on her bedroom door.

She was out in the hallway in three minutes, wearing a fresh change of clothes and carrying my overnight bag. She wore a stocking cap on her head so she wouldn't need to take time to fix her hair. How can I feel anything but love for this great lady?

Bob hit the Uber app on his phone, a maneuver he'd practiced many times. We went out to the curb and the car was waiting for us. Tilly sat between Jane and me and Bob rode in the front seat next to the driver.

We arrived at the hospital a half hour later, but it seemed more like two hours. My contractions were coming a bit faster. Maybe it's because we're a bit old fashioned even though we're young, but we didn't look at the ultrasound which would have told us the gender of the baby. We wanted to be surprised when the doctor said, "It's a boy," or "It's a girl."

At 7:20 a.m. we got our answer. "It's a boy!" Doctor Wagner announced. For nine months I'd been wondering what it would feel like when my new baby was handed to me to snuggle. It can only be described as a peak experience. Bob put his big arms around me and James Edward Nelson-Lawton as Jane snapped photos from her phone. Then Jane and Tilly posed on either side of me and the baby as Bob took pictures. Then the nurse photographed the four of us. I'd never seen Tilly look so happy as she stroked her little brother's head. As I looked at her and baby James my heart melted.

I was tired, but not so tired that I didn't stop baby talking constantly. Bob reminded me that we had resolved not to use baby talk when communicating with our new child, just as we avoided it with Tilly. But when I looked down at James, I thought he was the most beautiful human being I'd ever seen—of course. I couldn't resist letting go of a few "coochie-coos."

I let go of all the upsetting shit that we'd been through recently with the Long Island quarantine and luxuriated in the warm glow of being a brand-new mother.

"You have a visitor, Bobbie, if that's okay with you," Nurse Jackson said.

"Sure," I said, wanting to share this great moment with anyone who was kind enough to come visit.

"Congratulations, BBs!" the man said as he walked in wearing hospital scrubs.

"Oh, my God," both Bob and I yelled. "Commissioner Ralph! What happened?"

"I was kidnapped by the Solomon people, along with my staff."

"And they voluntarily let you go after the quarantine ended?" "Well, it wasn't exactly voluntary. One of the idiots left his gun on a table. It was quite a battle. I'm happy to say that we didn't lose anybody, and they lost all their people. I'll spare you the gory details for now in honor of this wonderful occasion."

"Please move over there, Commissioner," Jane said, pointing as she snapped more photos.

Bob put his head next to me as Jane chatted with Commissioner Norquist.

"So, now that you're no longer pregnant, are you over your dumb jealousy about Jane and our neighbor?"

"I admit I was stupid. But seeing you look at any woman in a bikini made me crazy."

"I have a question," Bob said. "Suppose you and I were sitting next to each other reading, which we often do, and a beautiful woman walked by. How would you feel if I lowered my head and kept on reading without looking at the woman? I am a healthy male after all."

I cracked up, totally getting Bob's point. "I'd order a few dozen doses of Viagra," I said laughing.

Commissioner Ralph said he had to leave and told Bob he looked forward to seeing him at One Police Plaza (One PP) the next day. I would be on maternity leave for another four weeks.

Jane took Tilly home, and Bob stayed with me and our new little James for a few more hours. Watching Bob with Tilly and now James makes me wonder how he got such a reputation as a tough guy. With kids, he's beyond gentle, almost like a cuddly panda bear. I love him to pieces.

The next day Bob would find out just how tough he'd need to be.

CHAPTER 43

Bob

I walked into One PP the Tuesday morning at 8 a.m. I felt like I was missing my right arm— Bobbie wasn't with me, and wouldn't be for a few more weeks of maternity leave. I had grown so accustomed to having Bobbie at my side that I felt like I was on a new job entirely. To me, Bobbie is more than a partner, she's part of me, and I'm part of her. I had just had breakfast with Bobbie, Jane, and Tilly. James, the newest addition to our family, was sleeping in his crib in our newly appointed nursery. As soon as I got to my office, 10 minutes after I left our apartment, I called to check in on them. Bobbie tells me that I'm like a new daddy on steroids I'm so overprotective. I don't care. My family means everything to me.

I walked into Commissioner Norquist's office at 8:30 a.m., and was surprised to see Sarah Watson, Director of the FBI, sitting in front of his desk. Sarah and I are old friends and we exchanged a hug. Sarah is famous for her bright smile, but her face looked serious, as did Ralph's.

"Congratulations on your new baby, Bob," Sarah said, a smile trying to assert itself. "Bobbie must be ecstatic. I'm going to drop by to visit her and the new baby after our meeting."

"That would make her happy as hell, Sarah," I said. "Bobbie's your biggest fan."

"While you were away on your forced vacation during that Long Island quarantine, Bob, the shit hit the fan here at One PP," Ralph said. "That's why Sarah is here. It isn't only hitting the fan here but at every law enforcement agency in the country. You know what I'm talking about, none other than that tyrannical scumbag Peter Solomon. We've never seen anything like him. I'm not exaggerating when I say that he's the most dangerous man in the country and his organization, that pack of Nazis known as the Committee of Freedom, is worse than the Mafia. General Bennet was smart as hell to order a military strike to end that Long Island quarantine, but as you know, our problems are far from over. They've only just begun. Sarah, why don't you fill Bob in on the latest."

"As you know, Bob, the major weapon of Solomon and his ilk is a thing called the Re-Education Project. The buildings in Montauk where the project operated from have been destroyed, but my sources on the ground tell me that they are conducting those bizarre programs at various locations throughout the country. The result is that we don't know who the enemy is. Not long ago we could identify people who were brainwashed by the way they spoke and acted, but that has all been changed. The new graduates of the Re-Education Project look and sound like normal people. The most serious problem is political. Peter Solomon wants to be President of the United States. Did you watch any of the nominating convention of the Committee of Freedom?"

"Yes, we watched the entire convention on TV."

"And what did you think about Peter Solomon's acceptance speech?"

"Frankly, Sarah, it scared the shit out of me. I decided to conduct a straw poll among the four of us and we all came to the same conclusion: Peter Solomon is a mesmerizing and convincing public speaker. He knows how to sway crowds, or at least crowds who don't listen carefully to what he says."

"Well, I'm about to tell you something that will not calm your nervous stomach. On all the evening news networks tonight they will announce a new Gallup poll. Half—that's fifty friggin percent, of the American people think that Peter Solomon would make a good president. Now, granted, neither the Democrats nor Republicans have yet to put up a candidate, but it's still astonishing that half the likely voters think positively about that goddam tyrant. Can you imagine what will become of this country if Solomon gets into the White House? It will no longer be the America that we love and trust. Your thoughts, Bob?"

"Yes, those Gallup numbers are upsetting, but I have a question. We're law enforcement people, and here we are talking politics, national politics. Is there something you're not telling me?"

"Shortly, Bob," Ralph Norquist said, "you're going to get a phone call from two people, two very powerful people. I can't tell you who they are, but you will find out shortly. They want to talk to you and Bobbie in the privacy of your apartment. The purpose of our meeting today is to let you know that you'll be getting that phone call. Sarah and I request that you give these guys a hearing, and to keep your mind open. I may be Commissioner of the NYPD and Sarah may be the Director of the FBI, but I'm here to tell you, the name Detective Bob Lawton rings bells around this country—Big, loud bells. They won't call you here to avoid any phone messages being traced, but you will get a call from Bobbie to convey the message. Here is the code word they will give Bobbie. Listen to these guys Bob, please listen."

I returned to my office. What the hell is going on? Ralph and

Sarah couldn't have been more cryptic. Two powerful men want to talk to me and Bobbie at our apartment? Something tells me that they're not editors wanting to talk about another book deal. Will my life ever get back to normal?

My phone rang. It was Bobbie, calling me to announce that she got the big phone call.

"They wouldn't give their names, Bob, but here is a codeword. Does that mean anything to you?"

"Yes, Ralph Norquist and Sarah Watson told me this would happen. The codeword they gave you is correct. Why don't you call them back and arrange for lunch at our place tomorrow?"

"Bob, do you have any idea what this is about?"

"Not a clue, not a friggin clue. See you later, honey."

CHAPTER 44

Bob

I didn't go to the office this morning because we'd be meeting with the two mystery men for lunch. I didn't sleep much last night, my mind busy pondering our mysterious upcoming meeting. Bobbie and I speculated nonstop as to what this meeting could be all about. At 11:30 the doorbell rang, and Jane answered it.

"Good morning, we're here to meet with Bob Lawton and Bobbie Nelson."

"We've been expecting you. My name is Jane. May I ask your names?"

"We'll tell the detectives that information,"

"Bob, Bobbie, your guests are here."

They walked into the apartment. Damn, I recognize these two, but I can't place them.

"Is it necessary that this young lady, Jane, be here?" said one of the two.

"Jane is our governess," I said. "When you have two little ones, domestic help is part of the program."

"Don't worry," Jane said. "I'll play with Tilly and James in the back room while you folks have lunch. I've prepared it already and it's on the stove." Leave it to Jane to immediately remove the stress from a situation. She took Tilly and James to the back room.

I put out my hand for a shake. "I'm sure you guys go by more than a codename. Mind if I ask who you are. You both look very familiar."

"I'm Roger Jones, Chairman of the Democratic National Committee and my colleague here is Blake Andrews, Chairman of the Republican National Committee."

"Is this a fundraiser?" I asked. I figured a wiseass crack would help thaw the atmosphere, and maybe calm the flips my stomach was doing. The two top political leaders in the country are here to see me. Me?

"Detective Lawton…"

"Please call me Bob, and my wife here is Bobbie. My I call you by your first names?"

"Of course," they both said.

We sat down to eat the steamed chicken casserole that Jane had prepared.

"My goodness," Roger Jones said. "this is delicious."

"Bobbie and I are good at hiring multitalented domestic assistance."

"I'll get right to the point, Bob," Blake Andrews said. "If you've been following the news, which I know you have, you have probably noticed that neither the Democratic nor the Republican parties have nominated someone to run for president, and the election is just over a year away. The only name in nomination right now is Peter Solomon, Chairman of the Committee of Freedom Party. "The most miserable scumbag on the planet," Roger Jones contributed. These guys like to get to the point.

"Most commentators say that the lack of a Democrat or Republican nominee is because of fear of what Solomon and his minions will do," Bobbie said. "Now I recognize you guys. I saw you two being interviewed by Bret Baier on *Fox.* Baier suggested that you both seem to fear running against Solomon. Neither of you would admit to fear, but you wouldn't deny it either."

"We'll be honest with you," Andrews said. "Yes, there is fear, but it's not just fear of violence, it's fear about not being able to raise sufficient funds and mount a credible campaign. Solomon has a huge and powerful political organization., with offices in all 50 states. Have you ever seen him speak in public?"

"Yes, I have, and he's as good in front of a camera as Roosevelt or Reagan. He's a mesmerizing speaker, and I know Bobbie agrees. We watched the convention along with a couple of friends. We did a straw poll after Solomon spoke and all four of us agreed that he's a dynamic public speaker with the power to get to people emotionally, even though all of us despise the bastard. I think that explains the weird Gallup poll which has 50 percent of the likely voters viewing him favorably."

"That's why we're so concerned and have decided to put aside our political disagreements and hold a joint convention of Democrats and Republicans to choose a candidate who we will cross endorse. Not to be dramatic, but the future of our country is on the line, if not our civilization."

"Pardon me, Blake, but what does all this have to do with Bobbie and me?"

"It has to do with you, Bob. Because of the strange circumstances we find ourselves in, we, both Democrats and Republicans, have decided to go outside the normal group of potential candidates, primarily politicians, and look for someone best described as a 'man of the people.' I'll get right to the bottom line, Bob, and our reason for being here. Roger and I are asking you to consider running for President of the United States."

Bobbie and I shared a glance, best described as "what the fuck?" Did I just hear correctly? These guys, representing the two major political parties, want me, Bob Lawton, to run for president? Am I asleep and having a weird dream? Bobbie and I spent six weeks locked up on Long Island during that quarantine, and I thought that now our lives would return to a semblance of normalcy. But now these two guys are talking about me running for president? Nothing normal about that. I got up and walked to the refrigerator to get a bottle of water. Truth was, I considered gin.

"From the look on your face, Bob, something tells me you haven't been considering this on your own," Roger said.

"Well, no. I can't imagine anything farther from my mind. Are you guys serious?"

"Yes, we're serious," Blake Andrews said. "Let's look at some objective facts, some objective characteristics about Detective Bob Lawton. You're a famous war hero, having received one of our country's highest decorations for valor, the Bronze Star. You put your life on the line and personally stopped the rifle company you commanded from being overrun. Your face is constantly on TV, along with your wife, talking about the major investigations you've conducted. You're extremely articulate, and not just when being interviewed on TV. I've seen recordings of speeches you've given at law enforcement conventions, and I'm here to tell you that you are one hell of a powerful public speaker. Also, you're a tall good-looking guy with an athletic build, and you cut quite a picture in front of a camera. Those traits will get the attention of women voters. In 2016, 63 percent of voters were women."

"Good looking? He's drop-dead gorgeous," Bobbie said, embarrassing me as usual.

"My wife totally agrees with you, Bobbie," Blake said. "I almost expect her to start a Bob Lawton fan club."

Bobbie reached over and squeezed my hand. Holy shit, can she be buying into this?

"To go further, your partner and wife here is just as good looking as you, causing many a man's heart to skip a beat. When you two are in front of a camera, two major demographics are addressed—men and women. And the two of you are known as the BBs, America's dynamic detective duo. Talk about branding! You've even written a best-selling book on the art and science of investigating crime, *Detectiving*. Also, Bob, you've written a best-selling police novel, *An Army of Blue*. You, Bob Lawton, are one class act."

"Blake and I agree that you will make a hell of a candidate. Please help us stop that evil bastard from ruining our country. The hour has come, and we want Bob Lawton to be the man of the hour."

Stunned doesn't begin to describe the way I felt. These guys want me, Bob Lawton, to run for President of the United States? This is definitely not what I expected this meeting to be about.

"I think you guys understand that Bobbie and I need to speak about all this," I said, trying to buy some time.

"Of course, and if you have any questions, and you will have them by the trainload I'm sure, feel free to call either of us about what's involved in running for president. This afternoon you're going to receive another phone call. I won't tell you who it is, but I think you will learn that Roger and I aren't your only cheerleaders."

After Drake and Roger left, Bobbie and I sat staring at each other.

"I'm not sure I can even believe what just happened," I said. "Hey, I'm a cop, maybe a good one, but what the hell do I know about running a country?"

"Don't be so humble, Bob. There's an elusive quality about you I think military people call a *Command Presence*. It probably comes from your brave leadership that got you awarded that medal. I've noticed that in countless meetings, not to mention crime scenes, when Bob Lawton speaks, people shut up and listen. And I wasn't kidding when I said you're drop-dead gorgeous. As Roger pointed out, the majority of voters in the country are women, and you will have their undivided attention. I know you have mine. Although it pisses me off, I've heard countless lady cops refer to you as a panty dropper. Always works with me. Bob, those two powerful political leaders wouldn't come calling if they didn't think you're the man for the job. I love you, honey. You're the man to lead us out of this shit. Peter Solomon won't know what hit him. Hey, let's get Jane in here. We haven't been sworn to secrecy, and I'd love to hear her opinion."

Bobbie walked to the back room. Tilly and James were napping, so she whispered to Jane that we'd like to have a cup of coffee with her.

"Those two guys looked awfully familiar," Jane said. "I think I've seen them on TV."

"They're the respective chairman of the Democratic and Republican National Committees," Bobbie said.

"Wow, since when do donkeys and elephants pal around?"

"When they find something they can agree on, and they have—Bob."

"What? Can you be a bit less cryptic, Bobbie?"

"They want Bob to run for President of the United States, and they intend to cross endorse him."

"Holy shit!" Jane squealed, causing Lucky to bark, as she wrapped her arms around my neck. "Bob, you're the perfect man for the job. I've always thought you were cut out for bigger things. Oh my God, President Bob Lawton. This is just fabulous. I can't wait to tell Steve. He'll freak out, just like I'm doing. And you're going to need an attentive governess in the White House, hint, hint," she added. Then she broke down in tears. "Please say yes, Bob," she said between choking sobs. "I've been a fan of yours for longer than I can remember—and now I'll get to vote for you. Oh my God, our country needs you. Please say yes."

The phone rang and Jane picked it up. Her eyes were like softballs.

"Yes, yes, of course, sir. He's right here. I'll put him on."

"It's the president," Jane said, looking like she was about to fall over. "He wants to speak to you, Bob."

"The president of what?"

"The President of the friggin United States." She sat next to Bobbie on the couch and they held hands, staring at me.

"Good afternoon, Mr. President, Bob Lawton here."

"Bob, we've met before, when I proudly awarded you and Bobbie with the Medal of Freedom for your fantastic work in law enforcement. I had a long meeting with Roger Jones and Blake Andrews. They're both one hundred percent in agreement that they want to cross endorse you to be our next president. It isn't often that the top Democrat and top Republican agree on something, but they have. And I agree with them too. You're one hell of a tough guy, Bob Lawton, and that's just what we need in the Oval Office. Peter Solomon and his slavish followers want to take our great country to a dark place. Bob Lawton won't let that happen. And Bobbie will make the perfect first lady. She reminds me of Meg, a strong woman not unaccustomed to leadership.

"Bob, I know you've just been hit with this idea, and I won't put you on the spot by asking for your answer right now. But please decide by tomorrow. Call me personally and I'll let Jones and Andrews know about your decision. Bob, please let your decision be a yes. You owe it to our great country. I'll talk to you tomorrow."

I had taken the call standing up as I always do when it's an important call. And I guess a call from President Fenton ranks as important. Bobbie and Jane both ran to me and wrapped their arms around me. "Yes, yes, yes," Jane yelled, "tell the man yes."

"What do you think, Bobbie?"

"As far as I'm concerned it's a go, honey, oh my God is it a go. I can't think of a better candidate," she said as she squeezed my hand, tears streaming down her face.

"That's all I needed to hear, baby. If it works for you, I'll make it work for me."

"Not to mention the country," Jane added. Then she handed me the phone. "Hey, enough with this political foreplay. Why don't you call President Fenton right now and tell him you're in?"

I did just that.

I began this day by leafing through files of cases we were

investigating. And now I'd just agreed to run for President of the United States.

Interesting day.

CHAPTER 45

Gloria Wetherill walked into Chairman Peter Solomon's private office at 8:45 a.m. She wore her usual skintight short skirt and a light knit cardigan sweater buttoned up almost to her neck. As soon as Solomon walked in, she removed her cardigan, revealing more than the usual display of cleavage above her form fitting yellow blouse. The chairman, she noticed, seemed more than usually aroused. She wondered if he was taking Viagra to boost his stamina. She wished she could find some kind of pill to give her a little enjoyment during their increasingly frequent bouts of dull sex. But, she reminded herself, she had an objective and it had nothing to do with pleasure. Her objective was power, and what better way to achieve power than controlling the most powerful man in the world. This was her project, plain and simple.

"So, Gloria, please update me on out political plans, but more specifically, the plans of the Democrats and Republicans." As he spoke, he walked over to her and gently stroked the top of her breasts.

"I have some interesting news from a few of our inside sources, Mr. Chairman," she said, batting her eyelashes in her practiced "alluring" look. Gloria regularly met with a group of six men who she thought of as insiders, her insiders, people who fed her secret information so she could impress the chairman. The insiders were happy to feed Gloria the information, because she fed them the hottest sex they could ever imagine. Gloria prided herself on the use of her stunning body.

"I have received information that the Democrats and Republicans are discussing a joint political campaign, united behind a candidate who both parties will cross endorse. Although the latest Gallup poll is quite encouraging, giving you 50 percent of the popular vote, that could change dramatically if a candidate comes forth with a cross endorsement, especially with the huge majority of likely voters controlled by the two major parties."

"Do you have any idea of the identity of this potential candidate, Gloria?"

"As of now I have no idea who it is, but I'm working on it, Mr. Chairman. I'm working on it diligently." As she said the word "diligently," she reached up and gently stroked his crotch. She felt him becoming aroused.

"I think some vigorous exercise will help you keep your mind diligently focused," he said as he reached down and pulled her blouse over her head.

Great, she thought, another hour of boring sex is about to happen. She stood and wiggled out of her skirt. But a girl's gotta do what she's gotta do, she thought, as she knelt down in front of him.

CHAPTER 46

M r. Ronson, a woman named Mariella Smith is here to see you. She said something about a major contribution." Phillip Ronson was the Deputy Chairman of the Republican National Committee. Among other duties, Ronson was in charge of fundraising, including raising money for the upcoming joint convention of Democrats and Republicans.

Mariella Smith was the adopted name of Gloria Wetherill. She often used pseudonyms when acting under cover, or under the covers.

"Mr. Ronson, this is Mariella Smith."

Ronson's heart skipped a beat when Mariella Smith walked in. My God, this woman's got the hottest body I've seen in years.

She wore a tight-fitting suit with a short skirt. Her plunging neckline offered stunning view of full and beautiful breasts. She didn't want to appear obvious. Well, not *too* obvious.

Ronson extended his hand and she took it gently in both of hers, all the while engaging his eyes.

"It's a pleasure to meet you, Ms. Smith. Please have a seat."

"Please call me Mariella," she said softly as she crossed her long suntanned legs.

"Fine, Mariella, please call me Phillip. What can I do for you?"

"My superior, whose name I can't disclose just yet, is interested in making a sizeable donation to both the Republican and Democratic Parties for the upcoming election, in excess of five million."

"My goodness, that certainly is generous. Say, you look awfully familiar, Mariella," he lied, cautiously flirting. His wife had died two years before, and he was just dipping his toe into the dating scene. No way in hell could he avoid making a few awkward moves on this gorgeous woman.

"You've probably seen me at a few party meetings. I usually sit in the back. Philip, do you mind if I change the subject for a moment? I just need to say something that will totally embarrass me. I find you to be one of the handsomest men I've ever met. You cause my heart to flutter."

Holy shit, talk about a fluttering heart. He never thought of himself as particularly handsome, but so what. All that mattered at the moment was that this woman found him attractive.

"Well, thank you, Mariella. If I may say, you are one beautiful woman."

She gave him one of her well-practiced "alluring" looks.

"I'm sorry, Phillip, for being so forward, but I just needed to say that. You make me *hot*."

———

At 4:30 p.m., Phillip and Mariella/Gloria helped each other get dressed after an afternoon of seemingly nonstop sex. They also had a great conversation, everything from their personal backgrounds to politics, including potential candidates for the upcoming election. My God, Phillip thought, I'm 41years old and I've just had the greatest sex of my life.

"I hope I'll see you again, Mariella."

"Count on it, honey. You drive me wild."

He leaned down and kissed her, a hot, wet, we've-got-to-do-this-again-soon kind of kiss.

CHAPTER 47

Bobbie

Jane went out to do some shopping while Tilly and James napped. It was just Bob and me, surrounded by the realization that our lives had just gone through a seismic shift. Bob had just accepted an offer to run for President of the United States. I think I've loved Bob from the first time I laid eyes on him. He's big and tall, impossibly handsome, and the kindest man I've ever met. But besides love there is another thing I've noticed about the way I feel about him. I admire him, yes admire him. It's kind of nice to admire the one you love, but it's the truth. After we met with the two party chiefs, I told him that he has this elusive quality called "Command Presence." Simply put, people pay attention to Bob. He has a strength, a power, a sort of animal magnetism. And I don't just mean in bed, although he certainly shows it there. Just like Bob, I was surprised when the party chiefs offered him the opportunity to be the cross-endorsed standard bearer. I may have been surprised, but I wasn't shocked. Since that conversation, it dawned on me that nobody on this earth would make a better president than Bob. My Bob.

"Hey, a penny for your thoughts," Bob said as he walked into the room.

"You're going to need a lot of pennies, Bob. After our meeting with the party chiefs and your conversation with President Fenton, I thought, this is amazing. But then I realized there's nothing amazing about it. Bob Lawton for President of the United States? What a no-brainer, what a fucking no-brainer. You're it, baby, and you know what else?"

"What else?"

"We're going to enjoy this and have fun. Yes, fun."

He wrapped his arms around me.

"Only my positive thinking Bobbie could look at something as stressful as a political campaign and think of it as fun."

"Bob, honey, if there's one thing we know how to do is handle stress. And we have a wonderful bed for doing exactly that. C'mon, baby, let's go and destress."

"I feel more relaxed already."

"Don't relax too much."

CHAPTER 48

Something about the look on your face tells me my favorite aide has something important to tell me, Gloria," Peter Solomon said.

"Yes, sir, I do," she said, licking her upper lip, which always commands his attention.

It was a mild day, and they sat sipping coffee on the huge deck overlooking Utah Lake.

Gloria was wearing her usual low-cut blouse and short skirt. She kicked off her shoes, crossed her long legs and perched her dainty bare feet on Peter Solomon's leg. She paid close attention to Solomon's reaction to her. She knows he likes his private space, but she also realized that she was getting to him—as planned.

He stroked her leg, wanting the meeting to be over so they could get to more exciting things.

"So, tell me about your meeting in New York, Gloria," He said as he continued to stroke her leg.

"Oh, my God, Mr. Chairman, you're driving me wild."

Actually, she found his leg stroking to be extremely annoying, but of course she would never tell him that. He stopped stroking her leg so she could get her story out.

"What we've heard about the Democrats and Republicans planning to cross endorse a candidate is true, sir. Their plans are well underway, and it will be formally announced at a joint convention next month."

"Have they decided on a candidate?"

"Yes, they have."

"Well, don't be coy, Gloria, who is it?"

"Robert Lawton, better known as Bob Lawton."

"Who the hell is he? I've never heard of him."

Gloria reached into her briefcase and took out a sheaf of photographs and newspaper articles. She put them in front of him on the coffee table.

"Oh, yeah, that famous New York City detective. He and his wife Bobbie are known as the BBs. I've seen them interviewed on TV many times."

"The one and only, Mr. Chairman."

"You mean they're going to choose a cop to run against me?"

"Well, sir, he's a very famous cop and he has quite a following in both parties as I've learned. He's a highly decorated war hero and is an excellent a public speaker. He's also quite handsome, as you can see, a trait that resonates with female voters, who make up the majority of the electorate. We can't underestimate this man, Mr. Chairman."

"Gloria, you amaze me. You sure know how to do your research."

"Thank you, Mr. Chairman."

Yes, I know how to do my research. I also know how to fuck like a rabbit.

"Well, thanks to you, Gloria, we have an early warning about what is likely to occur. Any thoughts about our next plan of action?"

"Yes, sir. By the time the nominating convention is held, the American voters won't look at this guy as the sweet Boy Scout you see on TV. I've already started to line up women who will have some interesting stories to tell about the sainted Bob Lawton."

CHAPTER 49

Good evening ladies and gentlemen, I'm Norah O'Donnell for *CBS Evening News*. Our show this evening will be political history. For the first time ever, the Democrats and Republicans have decided to hold the first-ever joint nominating convention to pick a candidate to run for President of the United States, a person who will be cross endorsed in a historic first. Although the balloting hasn't begun yet, I'm going to discuss the most poorly kept secret in years. We expect that NYPD Detective Robert Lawton, known as Bob, will be the joint candidate of the Democrats and Republicans. The reason for this is simple, really. Both parties have found it difficult to find a traditional candidate to run against the controversial Peter Solomon, of the somewhat infamous Committee of Freedom Party, the newest political party in the land. We're going to take a brief station break and then I'll continue with my coverage.

"Welcome back, folks, Norah O'Donnell for *CBS Evening News* here."

She held her hand to her ear, a look of confusion on her face.

"Talk about political history. I've just been told that the first ballot has been held already, and the convention has been going on for only two hours. Let's go to the floor to hear the announcement. I see that Roger Jones, Chairman of the Democratic National Committee and Blake Andrews, Chairman of the Republican National Committee are about to make a joint announcement."

"Ladies and gentlemen," Roger Jones said, "It gives us great pleasure and honor to announce…"

"The next President of the United States," Andrews said.

"Bob Lawton." Jones said.

As if on cue, the crowd erupted into shouts and cheers. "Law-ton, Law-ton, Law-ton," they chanted.

Bob Lawton then introduced the man who agreed to be his running mate, General Mike Bennet. Given the circumstances Lawton wanted the man who would be a heartbeat away from the presidency to have a solid military background. Commandant of the Marine Corps fit the bill. Bob Lawton will never forget how Mike accepted his request.

"The only reason I'll take this job is because I'll be working for the finest man in this country, Bob. God knows, we need a tough grunt like you in the Oval Office."

When the cheering finally died down, the camera panned to Norah O'Donnell.

"As you folks know, we crazy journalists love to keep statistics. So, I can now report to you another piece of political history. You just heard the longest ovation for any candidate, including Franklin Roosevelt. Let's return to the convention floor to hear the acceptance speech by Bob Lawton."

In keeping with tradition, Bob and Bobbie walked around the platform waving, their hands locked together.

Bobbie stood next to Bob as he gave his speech. "The BBs are a team, and we should stand together," Bob had told her. But it wasn't only their idea. The floor manager suggested it, thinking that the stunningly beautiful Bobbie Nelson standing next to her husband would add to the optics of the event.

"Ladies and gentlemen, to say that I'm honored is a vast understatement," Bob began. "I stand here next to my wife, my partner, the mother of my children, the best part of my life. As you know, I'm a cop, and so is Bobbie. But don't worry, neither of us is armed." That brought a few laughs.

"Bobbie and I have become known as the BBs, a phrase that I love, and the reason I love it is because it describes how close we are. We will now bring that same closeness to the Oval Office. But this isn't the general election, and a lot of work needs to get done to make sure the White House isn't occupied by a tyrant. You know who I mean."

More applause.

"Our nation is going through difficult times, to say the least. From the infamous quarantine of Long Island, to the constant reports of people being brainwashed, this is a difficult part of our history. While we can't rewrite history, we can make sure that the future holds the potential we've grown to expect from this great country. So, I make you a promise, and Bobbie shares in that promise. We won't let you down."

Another standing ovation, this one lasting for 10 minutes.

The camera panned back to Norah O'Donnell.

"So, there you have it, a historic cross endorsement by the Democrats and the Republicans, nominating a man, who until recently, lived in relative obscurity, except for his TV appearances discussing his cases. I have personally interviewed Bob and Bobbie on countless occasions. I will say this about both of them. When you talk to the BBs you are talking to the real deal. No evasiveness, no puffery, no nonsense. I ask a question and it gets answered. I hope my producer doesn't have a coronary when I say what I'm about to say. Given that this honorable man's opponent is the epitome of evil, I don't hesitate to say that I look forward to voting for Bob Lawton in November, and I urge you to do the same. Let's send the BBs to the White House."

CHAPTER 50

Bob

Holy shit. Norah O'Donnell publicly endorsed me on national TV. TV anchors may hint at who they're in favor of, but she flat out endorsed me. And she wasn't fired! Peter Solomon may have some fans, but not fans with brains and a following like Norah O'Donnell.

Bobbie and I were about to meet with Mike Simon, my campaign chairman. He was highly recommended by both Roger Jones and Blake Andrews, so who was I to object? Those guys know a lot more about electoral politics than I do. Mike had run or worked on six presidential campaigns, and everyone said he's an expert, and enthusiastic as hell.

"I'm about to start your day with good news," Mike said. "The average of the latest polls have you ahead at 65 percent. While it's still early, that's an excellent lead. Bob, you did one hell of a job at the convention. You are one great public speaker, my friend. So now for the bad news."

"Bad news?" Bobbie said.

"Yeah, really shitty news. As you know, we have some spies watching over the activities of the Committee of Freedom. Bobbie, if you believe the news you'll read over the next few days, you will think that you married a sexual deviate, a pervert at best. Bob is going to be smeared like peanut butter on toast, with accusations of various sexual misdeeds, including stories from underage children."

"What can we do about it?" I asked.

"We're going to come out with two guns blasting. As soon as a story hits, you will go public with an immediate denial. One fortunate thing we have going for us is that news people are in your corner, Bob. You heard Norah O'Donnell at the convention, openly endorsing you. To say that blew me away is an understatement. Your good friend, or I should say *our* good friend, Dr. Bennie Weinberg has been doing a great job of identifying people who went through that goddam Re-Education Project. He is mainly concentrating on news people and neutralizing them with that Torlazine stuff if he determines that they have been zombified. The next few months will be difficult, I hate to tell you, but besides being America's favorite lovebirds, I know that you're both tough as nails. And you're going to need to be tough when the crap is hurled at you. My spies tell me that an article will appear tomorrow claiming that your new little boy, James, is illegitimate, the result of Bobbie screwing some stranger."

"They wouldn't dare," Bobbie said.

"Yes, they would, and that's only the beginning of it. Keep in mind that those people are evil, pure evil. Expect to see Girl Scouts in brigade strength telling lies about Bob. Nothing will slow them down in their attempt to derail Bob's campaign. Expect to see some weird shit in the next few days."

CHAPTER 51

Bob

I sat in my office at One Police Plaza reviewing case files with Jason Bitterman and Walter Langone, the detectives who would take over for Bobbie and me while we're on leave of absence to work on my presidential campaign.

"I hope to hell that this will be our new office permanently, Bob," Jason said, "not just for my career but because that will mean you've traded in this place for the Oval Office."

"I second what Jason just said," Walter chimed in. "I think you will be one hell of a great president. I'm honored that Commissioner Ralph chose us to fill in for you two. I don't know if we'll ever be the BBs, but we'll give it a shot."

I really liked these two guys, and I think they'll do a great job. They had just gotten a call to report to a crime scene. I planned to stay in my office for about an hour, dictating memos to help my replacements. After that I planned to meet with Bobbie and Mike Simon, my campaign chairman, at the Lawton for President headquarters on 49th Street.

My phone rang. "There's a woman named Alexis Montrove here to see you, Bob. She says she's from the *Boston Herald*, and would like you to give her a brief interview. She apologized for not calling in advance. I checked with the *Boston Herald*, and she's legit.

"Show her in, Betty, but I can't give her more than a half-hour."

Holy shit, what a knockout. By looking at her I couldn't tell if she was a reporter or someone interviewing for a screen role as the Happy Hooker. Her lovely tits were so prominently displayed that they looked like they were for sale. She had long shapely legs that were on full view beneath her short skirt.

My brain went on immediate alert. Mike Simon had warned me about women who looked like this. He said that it's common for an unscrupulous political opponent to send tempting eye candy to an opponent to sully his reputation. And Peter Solomon certainly fits the bill as unscrupulous. But my goodness, what a body. Can't hurt to look.

"As a journalist, I shouldn't say this Detective, but I can't help but be excited about your candidacy. You're a proven leader, and I must say, the most gorgeous man I've ever laid eyes on. Oh, I'm sorry, did I just say laid? I meant to say 'looked at.' You will be the handsomest president ever." Her "laid" crack was one of her favorite lines, one that always gets results.

I've had women flirt with me before, and I've learned to control the situation. But I've never encountered a woman quite so forward. Could she be a pro? Like a real pro, as in take-me-to- your-room-and-do-me-right-now kind of pro?

As a long-time detective I have an innate sense when something isn't right. And something definitely was not right with this chick.

"Pardon me but I just got a text," I lied as I took a photo of her with my cellphone. Maybe Mike Simon will recognize her. He is beyond thorough when it comes to knowing who the actors are in politics.

"I'm sorry, Ms. Montrove, but I really must be going to my campaign headquarters. Perhaps we can reschedule an interview there next week sometime."

"Please call me Alexis. And I can think of other places where we could meet for a serious interview," she said, with her carefully practiced alluring smile.

"Please call Lawton for President headquarters and they will be happy to schedule an interview. Sorry, but I really must be going. Have a nice day, Alexis."

She batted her beautiful eyelashes at me. Could this be rehearsed?

———————————

A half hour later I walked into my office at campaign headquarters. Bobbie and Mike Simon were waiting for me. I shook Mike's hand and gave Bobbie a hug, a tight hug, a you-are-my-woman-and-I-love-you hug.

"Missed me? It's only been a few hours," I said.

"Yes, more than you know."

"Hey, why don't I let you guys be. We can meet later," Mike said, laughing.

"Get used to us, Mike, we're like this all the time," Bobbie said.

"Hey, Bob, you look troubled by something," Mike said.

"I just had an unscheduled interview with a reporter. She said she was from the *Boston Herald*. But something tells me it wasn't right."

"Did she jump you and profess her undying love for you?" Bobbie said, laughing.

"Almost," I said. Bobbie stopped laughing.

I clicked on the photo of Alexis Montrove and handed it to Mike. "Ever seen this lady, Mike?"

He handed the phone to Bobbie, who said, "Holy shit."

"Yes, I've seen her many times," Mike said. "Her name is Gloria Wetherill, not Alexis Montrove—and she's Peter Solomon's mistress."

This time Bobbie and I performed a duet of "holy shit."

I then explained her journalistic flirting, including the detail that she wanted to meet me anywhere other than headquarters.

"So, how did the interview end up?" Bobbie said, looking pissed.

"We're running away next week to get secretly married."

"Wiseass," she said, cracking up as she slapped my arm.

"Are you sure she's who you say she is, Mike?"

He reached over and looked at the photo on my phone again.

"Yes, that's definitely her. The last time I saw her she was blond, and now she's a redhead, but the same hairdo, the same short skirt with long legs, and the same come-and-get-it tits. This woman is dangerous, Bob, but she's seldom so clumsy. My insiders tell me she's power-driven and likes to control things around her, especially men, and most particularly Peter Solomon. Her picture should appear next to the words *femme fatale* in the encyclopedia."

"What should I say when she calls for another interview?"

"So, let me ask you a hypothetical question, Bob. What do you do with the plague?"

"Avoid it?"

"Exactly."

CHAPTER 52

Bob

Just as Mike Simon had predicted, a story hit the papers that our little son James was illegitimate, the result of Bobbie having slept with a stranger. We were amazed that none of the reporters who wrote the articles called Bobbie or me for a comment. Mike's spies told him that the reporters were insiders placed by the Committee of Freedom. Mike would make a good detective.

"Hey Bobbie, tell me about your secret lover with whom you conceived James."

She laughed and slapped my arm.

"So, what's your boyfriend like?"

"He's very short, extremely fat, but he has all the right moves. Wow, he is *HOT*."

"Do you see him regularly?"

"Yes, every day. Whenever I tell you I'm going to the property office or the records room, I go to the supply room and hump my fat

223

little boyfriend."

We both cracked up. Typical of Bobbie, she found a way to handle the rumors and lies that were being spread about me. Humor. There wasn't much more we could do other than joke about it.

As Mike Simon smartly recommended, I came out with an immediate denial when any made-up story about me appeared, including a signed statement from Bobbie's doctor explaining that DNA testing confirmed that James was my son.

The senior anchor people on all the networks, as well as the editors of newspapers all seem to share a common trait. They hate Peter Solomon. I don't know if they like me, but they sure don't like Peter Solomon. Bennie had done a thorough job of neutralizing the effects of the Re-Education Program and the vast majority of news people who had gone through the program, people who are now part of reality. But, as the story about James' supposed illegitimacy showed, there were plenty of reporters on the street who were in Solomon's pocket, or rather, Solomon was in their heads.

Gloria Wetherill, aka Alexis Montrove, called me constantly to try to set up an interview. Mike Simon turned his people loose and they quietly interrogated a couple of senior managers at the *Boston Herald*. We were amazed that Gloria Wetherill actually managed to land a job as a reporter for the *Herald*. As Mike reminds me, the woman is dangerous. She definitely knows how to use her hot body to get what she wants, and I didn't doubt that she used it to get her job at the paper. Her photo was circulated among my campaign staff, and the order was to call our security detail if she was seen at headquarters.

The weeks flew by fast. As a detective I'd grown accustomed to being busy, but the frenetic pace of a political campaign was new to me, and also new to Bobbie. Minutes blended into hours, hours to days, days to weeks. A long time ago both of us had taken up meditation, and we practiced it often on the campaign trail. We agreed that we needed to take some time off and, to use a strange word, relax.

It was time to head to East Hampton.

CHAPTER 53

Bobbie

The past three weeks have been insane. Bob would have a TV appearance one night and a speech to one group the next morning, then another one in the afternoon, and yet another that night. We both agreed that we needed to take some time off and go to East Hampton to chill. Mike Simon leased a huge Cadillac Escalade for us, along with a driver. On Friday morning we piled into the Escalade, along with our growing family, including Jane and her husband Steve. Steve has become a big fan of Bob's and he requested and was granted a one-year leave of absence from his job teaching at NYU so that he could work full-time on Bob's campaign. Apparently, Steve the financial whiz had salted away a few bucks. A job on a political campaign staff does not pay very well, certainly not as well as Steve's pay as an associate professor at NYU, which he supplements with constant gigs at management consulting. We were both impressed with Steve's intelligence and energy. Bob said that he wants to offer Steve a job on the White House staff. He always bounces his staffing ideas off me and I totally agreed with him. Steve living in Washington would enable Jane, our irreplaceable governess, to continue the job she loves in the White House. This isn't just family business, this is government business. Jane and Steve belong in the White House.

Our Secret Service detail, consisting of three men and one woman, followed us in another SUV. Our house in East Hampton had 10 bedrooms, which was a good thing because Bob and I tend to travel with a group wherever we go.

Tilly sat between Jane and Steve, with Lucky curled up on the floor. James sat in his car seat between Bob and me. I kept glancing over at Bob, noticing how gorgeous he looked that morning. Yes, he looked like a panty dropper, and that's exactly what I planned to do later.

As soon as we pulled up to our house, Maggie, the crazy Golden Retriever from next door, came running to us. We had alerted our Secret Service detail about Maggie, to make sure they didn't shoot her when she came charging at us.

Discretion is second nature to Secret Service people, and they politely refused our offer to have lunch with them. Bob insisted, however, and Jane prepared a huge feast as she always does so well. We enjoyed fried chicken, salmon steaks, potato salad, and cole slaw.

After lunch I announced that Bob and I were going to our suite to take a nap. Jane laughed. She knows that when we say "nap" it's a synonym for "screw."

After weeks of nonstop activity, I welcomed the chance to wrap my arms around my sexy husband. We undressed slowly, kissing all the time. Our bedroom suite is equipped with extra sound insulation, which is a good thing because Bob and I tend to make noisy love. Bob gently but persistently caressed my body, beginning with my breasts then moving down to my happy trigger. He slowly but deliberately brought me to my favorite place, the mountaintop. He joined me there as we reached a mind shattering mutual orgasm.

We lay there, our bodies entangled, as we caught our breaths.

"Love doesn't adequately describe how I feel about you, baby," I said, "but I can't come up with a better word so I'll just say it. I love you."

He wrapped me in his long muscular arms. "You just said my favorite words. I love you too, sweetheart."

We climbed out of bed and walked into the huge shower. Whoever designed this house was a very horny person. The shower stall included low platforms and cushioned benches, creating the possibilities of much more than bathing. And we did more than bathe. Much more.

When we reluctantly got out of the shower, we dressed in jeans and light sweaters. The mid-September air had a slight chill, aided by the breeze off Georgica Pond. We walked downstairs to the den, where Jane and Steve had just set up a Monopoly board. Tilly sat next to Jane, and James was in his springy baby sling.

"How was your nap?" Jane said, smiling.

"Perfect," I said, telling the absolute truth. Well, maybe not about the nap part.

Jane handed us the box containing the Monopoly pieces and said, "We just set the board up, so why don't you join us." Bob and I love to play Monopoly and we both said yes.

After two hours of playing the game, which Steve won, we decided to walk into town. Our Secret Service people walked discreetly a few feet in front of and behind us.

"I've got an idea," Jake Rubino, the head of the detail said, "Why don't you convince Mike Simon to make your campaign headquarters at your house." Like many visitors, our bodyguards fell in love with our house.

We reminisced with Jane and Steve about our strange stay in East Hampton during the Long Island quarantine, not a happy reminiscence.

"None of us will ever forget the Long Island quarantine," I said. "It was like a horror movie."

"Yeah, but it had a happy ending. What do you think Peter Solomon plans to do next?" Bob said.

"He plans to beat you in the race for president, Bob, but guess what? It's not going to happen—not as long as Bobbie Nelson's working the case."

CHAPTER 54

Committee of Freedom Chairman Peter Solomon convened a meeting of his key advisors in the general conference room at headquarters in Provo, Utah. As usual his aide and lover, Gloria Wetherill wasn't seated on the dais but in the back of the room. He preferred to keep their relationship discrete. He looked at her as he stood before the microphone. She ran her right hand across the top of her breasts, giving him a hint of what would come later.

"My campaign for the presidency is what we would expect at this point," Peter Solomon said to the crowd. "My opponent is ahead by 15 percentage points, but we have just begun to advertise. The Democrats and Republicans have chosen an interesting strategy. They have jointly nominated a man to run against me, and they cross endorsed him. The man's name is Robert Lawton, and he's a detective with the New York Police Department. He's little known except for his TV appearances when he's interviewed about one of his cases. His wife and partner is named Bobbie Nelson, and from what we've observed, they're a close couple. (And she's an outstanding piece of ass, he thought.) Detective Lawton is in for a few interesting months heading up to the general election.

"Not that we had anything to do with it," he lied, "but the Long

Island quarantine has come to an end as a result of military force. The Americans, in their typical clumsy way, believe that they can use force to achieve any result. But, to use an old phrase, they haven't seen anything yet. The Committee of Freedom is, indeed, the New World Order. The sooner the American political operatives realize that, the better off our country will be."

On cue, the crowd erupted in applause, a five-minute standing ovation.

"We have a lot of work ahead of us. With political offices set up in all 50 states, we're prepared to make this election turn out the way we want it to. That is all I have to say today. I'll be going into executive session in my private office. You will soon learn the results of our discussions."

Gloria bit her lip. When the chairman says "executive session," Gloria knows that he means a round of sex, a mind-numbing boring round of sex.

Gloria took the private elevator up to the chairman's private office on the upper floor. He was waiting for her.

"So, Gloria, what news do you have for me about my opponent?"

"As you know, sir, I have secured a job as a reporter with the *Boston Herald* through one of our inside operatives. I've adopted the pseudonym Alexis Montrove, and also Mariella Smith for some of my other undercover chores. I met only briefly with Detective Lawton, and have been trying to get an appointment for an interview since then. He doesn't return my calls. I think he may suspect something, so I've stopped calling to keep my identity hidden."

"And what is the latest you've learned about this man?"

"He's quite popular, although he's relatively unknown. That will change as the campaign moves forward. One disturbing thing is that he seems to be well-liked by the mainstream press. I was shocked to see the famous anchorwoman, Norah O'Donnell of *CBS,* come right out and endorse him the night of the joint political convention. That is unheard of. The fact that she wasn't fired tells us that senior management at *CBS* agrees with her. Our re-educated reporters are no longer-re-educated. Lawton has some powerful forces on his side."

"I believe you told me, Gloria, that we have reporters on the payroll who will be telling stories about Detective Lawton. Didn't I read a story that their new child was illegitimate, the result of Bobbie Nelson bedding a stranger?"

"That story became a laughingstock, especially after Lawton immediately released DNA testing showing that the child is his. I recommend, sir, that we be cautious in leaking stories. The mainstream press pounces on them."

"What are his major advantages, Gloria?"

"Well, as I've mentioned to you before, he's a highly decorated war hero, he's quite good looking, and he is a powerful public speaker, although nowhere near as powerful as you, Mr. Chairman."

"You say that he's good-looking. Do any of your women colleagues share your view?"

"Well, sir, there's only one man who has *my* eye," she said, batting her eyelashes as she had been practicing. "But I have overheard many women commenting on his good looks and athletic build. And women make up the majority of the electorate."

"Gloria, I'm quite impressed with your diligent spying. How do you do it?"

"I keep very careful records, sir." (And also, I know how to fuck to get what I want).

"Keep up the good work."

"If I may say so, sir, you seem to be under a lot of stress."

"Any thoughts on how to help me with my stress?"

She stood and began to unbutton her blouse. When it fell to the floor, she removed her skirt, kicked off her shoes, and walked over to him. "Just relax, Mr. Chairman. Let me take care of your stress." She slipped off her thong, tossed it on the floor, and stretched out naked in front of him on his desk. This is going exactly as planned, she thought.

CHAPTER 55

Bob

I met with Mike Simon and Bobbie in my office at Lawton Campaign Headquarters on 49ᵗʰ Street. The general election is three weeks away, and I'd be lying if I said I wasn't nervous. I may be a political novice, but with Mike and Bobbie, I don't feel the need for any other advisors. Bobbie, one of the most intelligent people I've ever known, is totally on top of the literature about running a political campaign. She also gives me strength and seems to know what I need to do at any time. Just another reason to love her.

In the next week, I have 10 TV interviews and seven planned speeches. I'm ahead in the polls with a 15-point lead. Mike tells me it's an excellent lead, but why don't I feel excellent? I have a hard time wrapping my head around the idea that there are voters who actually want Peter Solomon as president. Unfortunately, a lot of Americans watch sit-coms rather than the news and read cheap novels rather than newspapers. Peter Solomon, our leader and savior? Holy shit.

Bobbie and I walked into Mike's office, holding hands. When I'm near Bobbie, I find it impossible not to hold her hand. Just the touch of her skin centers me, and I definitely needed centering.

"Bob, I've been in the game a long time, and therefore I don't make predictions I can't believe in. But I feel confident that three weeks from now I'm going to be calling you Mr. President."

"Mike, at this point do you see anything going wrong?" Bobbie said.

"Not in the ordinary way of politics. Trends are trends, and the electorate is trending toward Bob in a big way. But our opponent is an evil son of a bitch, so I won't put anything past him. Bob, you and Bobbie stay close to your bodyguards, and keep your guns on you at all times."

Bobbie and I looked at each other. The thought intruded, based on what Mike just said, that one way for Solomon to pull this off is to have me assassinated. Not a pleasant thought.

At 7 p.m. Bobbie and I left the building and walked in front of my Secret Service detail to our waiting car. We held hands, of course. We heard a loud sound, and my left shoulder erupted in blinding pain. Bobbie reached to her waist, drew her Glock, and emptied it into a man who stood 15 feet from us holding a pistol, the one that just shot me. Eight Secret Service people surrounded us, their guns drawn as they scanned in all directions. I passed out.

I woke up in a hospital room with Bobbie standing next to my bed. A doctor was examining my shoulder. Four Secret Service agents stood by the door.

"I hate to say you were lucky to a man who has just been shot, but you *are* lucky, Detective. The bullet went through the soft tissue in your shoulder and neatly exited, leaving no serious damage. I'm happy for you, and I'm happy for the country. I look forward to voting for you in three weeks. You're going to be in quite a bit of pain for a while. Get some rest, Detective, or I should say, Mr. President."

Bobbie leaned over and kissed me after the doctor left. My Secret Service guys discreetly positioned themselves outside the door.

Bobbie was crying. This was the third time she'd saved my life.

"Bob, the thought of living without you is killing me. Maybe we should bag this shit and try to get our lives back to normal."

"Hey, honey, we made a simple mistake. We should always walk *behind* my Secret Service detail, not in front of them. No way in hell would I cede the election to that tyrant. By the way, that was quite nice of you to save my life."

"You *are* my life," Bobbie said.

CHAPTER 56

Gloria Wetherill stretched her long legs and perched her feet on the footrest on the chair in front of her in the first-class cabin of the Boeing 767. It was one hour from its destination in Canberra, Australia. She was travelling under the pseudonym Philomena Bates, a reporter for the *Canberra Times*. Wow, she recalled, it had taken her no less than three sleepovers with the editor-in-chief to nail that job.

She had an appointment to meet with Trevor Maltese, the newly-appointed Deputy Prime Minister of Australia. Her careful research told her that he is the wealthiest man in Australia with a net worth of over $15 billion dollars American.

Trevor Maltese was Gloria's next project.

Peter Solomon, her former boss who thought he was her lover, is well-done toast, she surmised. His Long Island Project had turned out to be a debacle, with the Americans bringing it to a sudden end with a military strike. That was followed by the cross endorsement of that unknown detective, Robert Lawton. Assuming he's elected president, which seems likely, with Lawton's impeccable law enforcement credentials, she expected to see indictments to flow like a river against the people involved in the Committee of Freedom.

Without leadership, the re-educated zombies would have nothing to do. All in all, however, her Peter Solomon project turned out to be successful. She had accumulated a sum of $12 million in a bank account in the Cayman Islands. Peter Solomon always showed his appreciation of Gloria's attention to every detail. But now he was history, her history.

A tall, somewhat good-looking man walked up to her and, gesturing to the empty seat next to her, said, "Mind if I sit so we can chat?"

The last thing she wanted was a dalliance with a stranger when she had a major project to work on, but she figured a little practice couldn't hurt. The man, who introduced himself as Dirk, immediately complimented her on her figure while staring at her legs and bare feet. Dirk, who was so forward it was almost humorous, proceeded to flirt like a teenager. As the plane began its final approach, he said he would like to spend an evening with her. "Sure," she said, practicing her alluring smile as she handed him a phony business card. "Call me tonight after seven." She chuckled to herself as to what his reaction would be when he found that the phone number did not exist.

After she checked into her hotel, she showered and put on her short skirt and tight blouse. She wore high heels, which helped to accentuate her stunning legs. At two in the afternoon, Gloria walked into the Department of the Prime Minister and Cabinet for her scheduled "interview" with Trevor Maltese. She stopped in the ladies' room and looked in the mirror. She carefully unbuttoned the top two buttons of her blouse and leaned forward to make sure her breasts signaled welcome.

Trevor Maltese took a quick deep breath when his assistant showed in Gloria, aka Philomena. *My goodness, this woman is* beautiful he thought. She reached over to shake his hand, letting her grasp linger for a few moments. Having divorced the year before, Maltese found himself often staring at women, especially women with gorgeous bodies. The article she was supposedly working on was about the Deputy Prime Minister's thoughts on his first few days in office. As he spoke, she stared into his eyes with her well-practiced alluring face.

"I'm afraid I'm going to embarrass myself, but I must say you are one of the handsomest men I've ever laid eyes on. Oh, I'm sorry, did I use the word *laid*?" Her favorite line always gets results, and from the look on Trevor's face, she expected a solid win. Nothing like a little sexual double entendre to get a meeting off to a good start.

That night, after they made love and she lay naked next to him, she said: "I've always thought it must be fascinating to work in government with a serious leader like you. By any chance would you have an opening for an aide?" she said as she stroked his chest.

"When can you start?" Trevor said.

Gloria's latest project was well on its way.

CHAPTER 57

Bob

The day before election day, Bobbie and I sat with our attorney to revise our wills. Nothing like taking a bullet to remind you that life can be fleeting. After we consulted with Jane and Steve (and they readily agreed, God bless them), we put them down as our choice of guardians for Tilly and James, as well as Lucky the bulldog. We also arranged for a huge trust fund to take care of their needs.

The next day Bobbie and I voted at our local polling place at 6:30 a.m. My shoulder hurt like a bitch, but I didn't want to be stoned with painkillers, so I just put up with it, popping an occasional Tylenol. Bobbie, no surprise, knew just where to massage the base of my neck to ease the pain.

We went to Lawton Campaign Headquarters to meet Jane and Steve, and Tilly and James for breakfast. It was eight in the morning, and we had a long day before us. Mike had assigned a group of campaign workers to do exit polling throughout the day. Mike was impressed with Steve Rankin, Jane's husband and new member of my campaign staff. I'm definitely going to offer Steve a White House job, assuming I win of course. Mike put Steve in charge of the poll monitors, an important post. The numbers looked good, although the polls in the East wouldn't close until 9 p.m. Will the closing of the polls see me as the new President of the United States, or will we find ourselves suddenly living under a tyranny? The evidence looked clear that I'd be the winner, but the detective in me reminded myself not to trust the evidence until it became conclusive.

General Mike was already there with his two brothers and a sister, and a tall pretty woman named Liz Baker, whom he'd been seeing recently. Although there's nothing in the Constitution that says a vice president can't date, I intend to recommend that he ask for the woman's hand in marriage. I'd met her a few times, and she's a damn fine woman, intelligent with a great sense of humor, not to mention quite good looking. She's 43 but looks ten years younger. I'm sure the widower General Mike will like the idea. I have as feeling that he's been thinking about just that for a while.

I looked at my watch. Five minutes till nine p.m. My shoulder stopped hurting, replaced by a burning knot in my stomach.

Bobbie, Mike Simon and I stood in an area surrounded by TV sets, all tuned to different networks, including *ABC, CBS, NBC, CNN,* and *Fox.* I felt like my entire life focused down to that moment.

Holy shit. At the stroke of nine o'clock, all five networks called the election for me. I won 79 percent of the popular vote and a clean sweep in the electoral college, a huge landslide by both counts, and the final numbers aren't in yet.

I'd just been elected President of the United States.

The room broke out into expected happy bedlam. I was shortly to give my acceptance speech, which I wrote with Bobbie. But first, I just wanted to be with the most important person in my life.

Bobbie hugged me so closely you couldn't tell where she stopped and I began. We stared into each other's eyes as confetti piled up on our heads.

"We did it, baby," I said. "Are you at all concerned about what life will be like in the White House?"

"Not a bit, not even a tiny bit."

"I'm glad to hear you're not at all concerned. Typical positive thinking Bobbie. But why aren't you worried, even a little bit?"

"We'll be together."

The Long Island Project

Characters – *The Long Island Project*

Andrews, Blake – Chairman of the Republican National Committee

Arkin, Randy – Astronaut, Space Station Liberty

Bateman, Jenny – CEO, Robot Depot

Bennet, Mike – General, Commandant of the United States Marine Corps

Blake, Jim – SCPD bodyguard

Bracken, Frank – East Hampton Police Chief

Brown, Loretta – Astronaut, Space Station Liberty

Conklin, Jim – History Professor

Crowley, Stan – NYPD Detective – The Resistor

Cummings, Grant – General Manager of the Venetian Hotel

Drummond, Victor – Lt. Colonel, Committee of Freedom

Jones, Roger – Chairman of the Democratic National Committee

Langdon, Drake – FBI Agent

Lawton, Bob – Detective, NYPD, Bobbie Nelson's husband

Lipton, Walter – ABC News Anchor

Lombardi, Tony – SCPD bodyguard

Lucky – A French Bulldog

Maggie – A Golden Retriever, friend of Lucky

Montrove, Alexis – Pseudonym for Gloria Wetherill

Nelson, Bobbie – Detective, NYPD, Bob Lawton's wife

Patton, Rick – FBI agent

Porter, Ronald – CBS News Anchor

Rankin, Steve – Jane Romelli's fiancé

Remington, Dennis – US Army Major

Remington, Liz - US Army Lieutenant, wife of Dennis

Romelli, Jane – Tilly's governess

Ronson, Phillip – Deputy Chairman of the Republican Party

Simon, Mike – Political Campaign Manager

Smith, Mariella – Pseudonym for Gloria Wetherill

Solomon, John – Executive Officer, *USS Eldridge*

Solomon, Peter – Chairman, the Committee of Freedom

Stratton, Jake – Peter Solomon's running mate

Townsend, Mike – Suffolk County Police Commissioner

Weinberg, Bennie – Detective and psychiatrist

Weinberg, Maggie – Criminology professor, Bennie's wife

Wetherill, Gloria – Aide to Committee of Freedom Chairman Solomon

THE BOOKS OF RUSS MORAN

I hope you enjoyed reading *The Long Island Project as* much as I enjoyed writing it. As many a Long Islander, I have spent time "stuck" on Long Island, the result of a traffic jam. I'll never forget the time when the Verrazano Bridge, the Throgs Neck Bridge, the Whitestone Bridge, and the George Washington bridge were all shut down hard. As I drummed my fingers on the steering wheel, I did what most novelists do – I looked for a story, or rather I noticed that a story had found me. What if Long Island was quarantined with no way on or off? By the time I eventually found my way to New Jersey, a story had formed in my head, *The Long Island Project*.

This book, as well as all my books are available on Amazon. com, and also as ebooks on The Kindle or a Kindle app on your smartphone or iPad.

The Gray Ship – Book One of *The Time Magnet Series*
http://amzn.to/16GPumH

A number one Amazon best seller. "This provocative, intensely powerful novel is a must-read for sci-fi fans and Civil War aficionados, though mainstream fiction readers will find it heart-rending and inspiring as well. A rare read that's not only *wildly entertaining, but also profoundly moving*." – Kirkus Reviews

The Thanksgiving Gang – Book Two of *The Time Magnet Series*
http://amzn.to/1NzBs7N

The Sequel to *The Gray Ship*. A story of time travel.

"I had never read a book before written in an efficient, minimalistic prose. Instead of writing what most readers want to read, he gives voice to life-like characters, with their flaws and prejudices. They are not infallible superheroes. It's always nice to find a new voice in fiction and to enjoy creativity at its best." — C. Ludewig.

"Breakneck pacing and virtually nonstop action" – Kirkus Reviews

A Time of Fear – **Book Three of *The Time Magnet Series***
http://amzn.to/1zdjaG9

In a month, five American cities will be devastated by suitcase nuclear bombs.

The time travelers take on their old name, *The Thanksgiving Gang*.

-They know what will happen, because they travelled to the future.

-They know what the result will be. They've seen the devastation.

-They know the details. Five American Cities targeted by nuclear suitcase bombs.

-BUT they don't know where the bombs are—and they don't know how to find them.

The clock is ticking, and millions will soon lose their lives – unless they find the bombs.

"His story is fascinating, and adds even more depth to this already cavernously deep novel. Amazingly unique, chilling and well written, Moran weaves a future that is both desperate and hopeful. Blending modern fears with science fiction results in a tale that will keep you reading long into the night. Five stars!" – Heather

The Skies of Time – **Book Four of *The Time Magnet Series***
http://amzn.to/1CCC3jg

In *The Skies of Time*, you will recognize the two main characters, Ashley Patterson, now an admiral, and her husband, Jack Thurber. They met and fell in love in *The Gray Ship*, and now they're in for the adventure of their lives in *The Skies of Time*. Ashley and Jack have been such prominent characters in all four books of The Time Magnet Series that I feel like they're old friends. You will also recognize some of the other characters. But if I told you who they are, it would ruin the fun.

"I'm big fan of this series and this one may be the best. I hope there is another book to this series since it keeps getting better. There are a few questions I have about certain events that makes the next one even more suspenseful. These are great books to binge read one after the other." – Time Travel Fan

The Shadows of Terror – **Book One of the *Patterns Series***
http://amzn.to/1IDQzJS

A stunning page turner. A novel that explodes off the front page of your newspaper.

Terrorism has a new face, a face that's obscured in the shadows. The radical forces of destruction have learned to make themselves invisible to the West, and preventing a terrorist attack has become almost impossible.

A new war has begun, World War III.

Rick Bellamy, an FBI agent who specializes in counterterrorism, is engaged in his own war, a war with no end.

Bellamy's wife, Ellen, a prominent architect, discovers that she's in the middle of the greatest terror plot to date.

To defeat the enemy, Bellamy first has to uncover the clues, to shine a light on the shadows. He has to find patterns – before it's too late.

"Move over James Patterson and Mary Higgins Clark. There's a new guy in town. Russ Moran's new book – *The Shadows of Terror*." – Frank O.

The Scent of Revenge - Book Two in the *Patterns Series*
http://amzn.to/1UvDRmw

The world is at war with the forces of terror. FBI Agent Rick Bellamy and his wife, Ellen, find themselves in the middle of a sinister terrorist plot.

Someone is attacking young prominent women, inflicting a horrible disease.

Nobody knows its origin, nobody knows how to stop it, nobody knows how to cure it.

Rick Bellamy and a team of scientists want to go on the offense. But how?

Will the lives of the women be changed forever? When will the attacks stop?

"Heart pounding, can't put down thriller that will force you to look at terrorism in different light. Life in America will never be the same." – Cold Coffee Cafe

Sideswiped - Book One in the Matt Blake series of legal thrillers.
http://amzn.to/1MkxX35

Trial lawyer Matt Blake took on a perfect case.

It involved a sideswipe collision in which his client's husband, an investigative reporter, was killed. The evidence of negligence was overwhelming. Eyewitnesses testified that defendant was talking on his cell phone when he hit the other car.

But was it negligence? Was it an accident?

Or was it murder?

Matt uncovers evidence that the act may have been intentional. Somebody wanted the man silenced. Somebody wanted the man dead.

Somebody had a lot to hide.

The signs started to point to the highest levels of government.

An open-and-shut personal injury case suddenly became a vast conspiracy of terror.

"This book hooks you in from the first line. *Sideswiped* draws you into the world of Matt Blake and you become emotionally attached to him and his journey. The story itself is so well-written and moves quickly. There is never a dull moment." – Sarah Elle

"Moran demonstrates the depth of his writing talent by developing a new genre with *Sideswiped*, a legal thriller. Branching out from his previous novels dealing with time travel, Moran goes in a whole new direction with Book One in the Matt Blake series. He creates a wild but totally believable story of modern day intrigue and suspense. Moran also deftly weaves into this book some of my favorite characters from his prior novels. I am looking forward to starting Book #2 - *The Reformers* – Frank from Lynbrook on August 16, 2016

The Reformers - **Book Two of the Matt Blake Series of legal thrillers, is the sequel to** *Sideswiped.*
ttp://amzn.to/2m8uMdu

The forces of radical Islam are on the run.

Their leadership has been decimated, their ranks thinned, their power disappearing by the week.

Their recruiting efforts have been cut off, the radical websites shut down, and the attraction of jihad is losing its appeal among the young.

With targeted assassinations, military strikes, as well as the loss of oil fields and gold mines, radical Islam is fast losing power.

But who is responsible?

It isn't the United States Government. It's a new force the world has never seen before.

Lawyer Matt Blake and his wife Diana find themselves in the middle of the most gigantic plot the world has ever seen, a conspiracy that's only begun to grow.

"I've been a fan of the author, Russell Moran, since reading *Sideswiped* a few months ago, so I admittedly went into this book with quite high expectations. That being said, I had no idea that "*The Reformers*" was going to play out in the way that it does and I can see myself giving this book a re-read in the future. In fact, I am even more impressed by the storyline of this read than the last and it has left me excited to see more." – Lucidity.

The Keepers of Time - **Book Five of the** *Time Magnet Series*
http://amzn.to/2wjVSTt

Admiral Ashley Patterson and her husband Jack have done it

again. They've traveled through time, 200 years into the future –
aboard a nuclear aircraft carrier, Ashley's flagship.

They discover a new world, a strange new world – a post-nuclear
war world – one that is both a beacon of hope, and a cry of despair.

They meet a group of people who call themselves *The Keepers
of Time,* an organization dedicated to preserving history and culture
amid the horrors of a dystopian future.

The world around them has harkened back to a primitive and
savage past, one that includes human sacrifice.

Ashley knows they must have to get back to the present to warn
the government of the unspeakable horrors that await. But finding
the way back to the present is their greatest challenge, an almost
insurmountable one.

"The Keepers of Time is a really interesting take on current
geopolitical events and where they are leading. From reading
previous books in the series, the cast of characters is as familiar
as the people next door and it was great to reconnect with them.
Moran's legal background illuminates what happens when our legal
structure disappears, and he has zeroed in on an essential thing about
civilization – records of the past. A great read!" Robert Shearer

"Time flies when you're scared out of your mind. The author's
superb writing skills will quickly draw you into the story. Forty-
two fast paced chapters will keep turning the pages of this novel
until the end. Well-developed cast of realistic characters that you
will relate to one will keep you engaged. One of my favorite things
about Moran's books is his entire cast of characters detailed in the
back of the book. I admit to reading about the cast first in order to
firmly get everyone in my mind. As a follower of his, I know each
character is important to the plot and I don't want to miss anything
or overlook anyone." – Cold Coffee

"A wild time travel yarn that starts fast and doesn't slow down until the end."

A Reunion in Time
http://amzn.to/2tneIsg

What if a 37-year-old adult travels back 20 years in time and finds himself in high school, followed by his 36-year-old wife? They're now teenagers, 17 and 16.

Adults in teenage bodies, they struggle to convince the people from their past that they are real, not apparitions. With the benefit of hindsight, they know the history of the past 20 years, and it isn't pretty.

Rick and Ellen are married, and now have to adjust to married life as teenagers in 2001. Rick is a senior FBI official and Ellen is a famous architect.

But everybody sees them as kids. Nobody believes that they're married, and nobody believes their stories—until Rick and Ellen predict 9/11.

How do they find their way back to the year they came from? How do they warn the authorities of the cataclysm that will occur in the future? The answer is to find the time portal—the wormhole—that brought them to 2001. But the site has changed. It's no longer the place where they crossed the wormhole. Will they live out the balance of their lives beginning as teenagers?

"We've all wished we could go back to earlier times with the mind we have now. This Russell Moran book takes you there and it is a fun creative romp well worth reading. *A Reunion in Time* is highly recommend!" – Kindle Customer.

The President is Missing – Book Three of the Matt Blake series.
http://amzn.to/2t9v7wu

While he was addressing the nation from a submerged nuclear submarine, President Blake's message is suddenly cut off. Anyone listening heard an explosion. The explosion was followed by floating debris five minutes later.

First Lady Dee Blake has doubts, which she shares with naval high command and the new president. She thinks the explosion and the debris were a ruse to make people think the sub was destroyed, and her husband with it.

Could the sub have been hijacked and the president kidnapped?

But who would commit such an act? What is its purpose?

Was it Russia, China, Iran, or a shadowy group of freelance terrorists?

The new president appoints Dee as his Chief of Staff, with explicit instructions to find the missing submarine—and President Matt Blake.

Her life, and the life of the nation, suddenly take a horrifying turn.

"Russ Moran wrote a true thriller, with a strong plot and even stronger characters. To think that there are good guys - Russian Naval Admirals, no less - made this book not only a solid who-done-it but also a strong 'why did they do it?' " – Unka Heshie

Robot Depot
http://amzn.to/2zXW7C2

Mike Bateman is a visionary businessman, the creator and CEO of the fabulously successful chain of stores, Robot Depot, a company dedicated to selling robots and Artificial Intelligence machines for a variety of uses.

The company is a darling of Wall Street and is the most popular destination for consumers and businesses looking for labor saving devices.

But the company caught the eye of ISIS, the terrorist Islamic State. They discover a great way to deliver bombs – using the products of Robot Depot to kill people.

Robot Depot changed from being a popular company to an object of fear because of the tampered products it sells. The terrorists use the company for "terror spectaculars," including the destruction of a skyscraper, a drone attack on Yankee Stadium, and the bombing of a children's sailing regatta.

Mike Bateman and the FBI are in a race to stop his products from becoming weapons, a race to stop the wanton killings. His wife and partner, Jenny, discovers the true meaning of terror one horrible summer day.

"Moran just got a new fan. This is the first book of Moran's that I've read, but I look forward to reading more of his work. I enjoyed this story, and found that Moran is not only a good writer, but he's a good storyteller as well. It's an interesting and creative story, mixing new technology and AI uses, with terrorism. It's a thriller that keeps the reader turning the page, and it's extremely captivating. I enjoyed the story and look forward to future works of his." Amy's Bookshelf

A Climate of Doubt
https://amzn.to/2OSwcHR

Forget what you ever heard about climate change.

Forget your preconceived notions about reality itself.

Instantly, you are in a new world, a horrifying world, a world you don't understand.

On a hot summer day, Homeland Security Secretary, Rick Bellamy, and his wife Ellen, a famous TV talk show host, walked along the ocean front trying to escape the heat. Suddenly the temperature dropped from the high 90s to below freezing in a matter of minutes. It began to snow – *on July 16.*

The temperatures across the country and the world plummeted, creating winter in summer.

Bellamy and the rest of the government struggled to cope with the suddenly new climate, but to cope, they first had to find out what happened.

Scientists from academia blamed the weather on a sudden acceleration of climate change, but they were unable to explain a 60-degree temperature drop in a matter of minutes.

Two astronauts in an American space station realized that the sudden weather calamity coincided with a test of the 20 satellites that the space station controlled.

Attention focused on a huge American corporation that owned the space station and the satellites. Could there be a connection between the satellite tests and the radical drop in temperature?

As the deaths piled up and the world economy tilted toward disaster because of gigantic summer blizzards, Rick Bellamy and his team struggled to find answers before it was too late. Was it a sudden shift in climate change or did it have something to do with the satellites? The biggest question remained – was the catastrophe an accident, or was somebody controlling the weather? Was it terror?

Bundle up and get this page-turning thriller. You're in for a wild ride. The book was published in May of 2018. It's Book Four of the Matt Blake Series. Matt and Dee Blake take on their biggest challenge to date, along with our old friends, Rick and Ellen Bellamy.

"Mr. Moran does a masterful job of crafting an action-packed, suspenseful read about the devastating consequences of climate manipulation. The diabolical mastermind behind the caper is a dictator of the worst kind—a man without conscience who cares only for power. Through the magic of Mr. Moran's digital pen, the men and woman in white hats are three-dimensional and vividly real. While this is a work of fiction, it's plausible fiction. We can easily relate to the horrific consequences of such an act of terrorism as so capably portrayed in Mr. Moran's prose." – Colorado Avid Reader

***The Maltese Incident – A Story of Time Travel* (Book One of the Harry and Meg Series), the prequel to *The Violent Sea*.**
https://amzn.to/2RclZCT

You're on a beautiful cruise ship.

The April sky is full of stars.

Suddenly, the ship rumbles, and instantly the stars disappear.

"What the hell was that?" Captain Fenton yelled.

"Beats me, captain. I've never seen anything like it," the first officer said.

They would soon discover that the ship, *The Maltese*, had just traveled through time – millions of years to the past.

The captain, Harry Fenton, a highly decorated naval war hero, realizes the greatest battle of his life lay ahead of him.

Captain Harry, a widow, falls in love with a beautiful passenger, Meg Johnson, an executive with the company that owns the ship.

After a whirlwind romance, they marry – in the ship's ballroom—100 million years in the past.

Captain Harry convinces the passengers and crew that they must move ashore to a tropical island because the ship is running out of fuel and supplies. He organizes a group to go ashore and inspect the island.

An ancient forest inhabited by dinosaurs awaits them.

Meg wants to go with them. Harry, fearing for her safety, tries to convince her to stay on the ship.

Meg demonstrates that she is proficient with a gun by taking apart a rifle and reassembling it – in 15 seconds. Harry marvels that he's never seen such an expert gun handler – or accurate shooter. So, AR-15 in hand, Meg joins the inspection party. Charging dinosaurs are no match for Meg Fenton's firepower.

Will the 1,000 souls ever make it back to the time they came from, or will they remain stranded in the distant past?

A scientist aboard theorizes that, to return to their present time, they need to go back to the time portal, or wormhole, that brought them to the past.

But the ship doesn't have enough fuel for the journey.

Realizing that their lives have hit the reset button, the crew and passengers construct a community in the forest – Malta Town.

Under Harry and Meg's leadership, they create a court system, a legislature, and all the elements of a small budding democracy. Meg figures out a way to harness hydroelectric power from a nearby waterfall. Everybody thinks of Harry and Meg as the heart and soul of Malta Town. They begin their new lives – among the dinosaurs.

The Maltese Incident is a riveting tale of time travel, love, courage, and horror.

Get this page turner now and prepare for the ride of your life.

"As with Moran's work, he continues to be a great storyteller. I recommend reading this from title to end. It's well written, and filled with intensity and levity." – Amy's Bookshelf

The Violent Sea – A Story of Time Travel
Book Two of the *Harry and Meg Series,* the sequel to
The Maltese Incident.
https://amzn.to/2AT5ypI

The Violent Sea is a novel of war, time travel, military history. It's the second book in the Harry and Meg Series. It's also a sweet romance between Harry and his wife, Meg.

Rear Admiral Harry Fenton has done it again. He's traveled through time to a different era. He finds himself, with a serious head injury from a fall, at Pearl Harbor Base Hospital on May 16, 1942, three weeks before the Battle of Midway. His wife and aide, Lieutenant Meg Fenton, is worried sick, and waits for him—in 2018.

Admiral Harry is the commanding officer of Carrier Strike Group 14 in 2018, but the people in 1942 think he's a busted-up hallucinating sailor who imagines himself an admiral.

Admiral Raymond Spruance is commanding officer of Carrier Task Force 16. After hearing about Harry's time travel stories, Spruance orders him brought to his flagship, the *USS Enterprise*. After Harry tells him about his time travel experiences, Spruance is convinced the man is insane.

But after speaking to him at length, Spruance is amazed at Harry's knowledge of naval tactics and strategy. He calls Harry's bluff and orders him to stay aboard the *Enterprise* for her upcoming engagement at the Battle of Midway.

By the end of the battle, Spruance is convinced Harry is an admiral, and thinks of him as a friend.

Now Harry needs to figure out how to travel back to 2018, to his carrier command, but most importantly, to the love of his life, Lieutenant Meg.

After Harry returns to the present, the Fentons are deployed on Harry's flagship, the *USS Gerald R. Ford*. The ship encounters another wormhole, this one in the ocean. They are transported to 1944 and participate in the Battle of Leyte Gulf.

The book took me 10 months to write. It went through 20 drafts and three rounds with my editors. I did copious research for the book to ensure its historical accuracy. If you enjoy the genre of time travel, I think you will love this book. I got to know my two main characters in the prequel, *The Maltese Incident*. Harry and Meg are deeply in love but enjoy constant banter and wisecracks. One of my favorite characters, Admiral Ashley Patterson of *The Gray Ship,* makes an important cameo appearance in *The Violent Sea.*

"What a great book. You will love this book. Time travel telling at its best. At the end you will believe it is possible. Russell Moran has crafted a great continuation from *The Maltese Incident* his character development has continued from the first book throughout this book and possibly beyond. His writing is so detail oriented you will find yourself believing that time travel is not only real but possible. This book was given to me as a gift but it turned out to be one of the greatest gifts I have ever received. You will find that your investment of money and time reading this book to be a great investment. Time and money both well spent." – Mike the Mailman

A Sea of Fear – **A Novel of Time Travel**
Book 3 of The Harry and Meg Series.
https://amzn.to/2GERuSx

You're Five-Star Admiral Harry Fenton, whom President Blake calls the greatest fighting admiral in American history.

Along with your Navy Commander wife, Meg, you lead your carrier strike group against the worst enemy the country has faced since World War II, a small nation that is intent on destroying the world's shipping industry. The seas of the world have become scenes of plunder, pillage, and mass murder.

The president has convinced you to come out of retirement and put an end to the looming crisis. He promotes you to Fleet Admiral, the highest-ranking officer since Admiral Chester Nimitz.

You and Meg were having a pleasant retirement, running a world-class resort that you bought in Rhode Island. But when the president pleads you to "Give 'em Hell, Harry," you know that you can't ignore his call to duty.

As people who have time traveled in the past, you come up with an idea to travel three years into the future. With President Blake's blessing, you and Meg lead a group of officers into the future. What you find is horrifying, an America taken over by a totalitarian dictator.

You return to the past and report your findings. President Blake, hearing your terrifying story, convinces you that you have an even bigger call to duty, the greatest challenge of your life. You take on the challenge for one reason—Meg will be at your side.

As in the first two books of the Harry and Meg Series, *The Maltese Incident* and *The Violent Sea*, *A Sea of Fear* is a sweet romance between two of literature's most exciting and likable characters, Harry and Meg Fenton.

A Sea of Fear is a story of war, politics, time travel, and love.

"This story is incredible. I felt like it was real-life and happening NOW! The way the political world is unfolding with the lies and innuendos, something like this could be possible. The main couple, husband and wife, Meg and Harry worked together to solve and help the nation climb onto its rock-solid feet. Surely this is the integrity that the United States government stands for. They had me in their corner wanting to see them win against the evil Antonio Martin. Read the story, it will enthrall and pull you in as it did me...Great ending." – Cristella

Leonardo Murphy – A Coming of Age Thriller
https://amzn.to/31vzC4S

You just launched a satellite into space without a rocket.

You invented a computer algorithm that writes novels.

You just entered Harvard University on a full scholarship after completing high school in two years.

Not bad for a 12-year-old kid.

Leonardo changed his name from William to Leonardo to honor his hero, Leonardo da Vinci. Young Leonardo Murphy has the second highest IQ ever recorded.

Leonardo, now 25, met a beautiful young woman named Janice, and fell madly in love. They married a year later.

Janice and Leonardo, who she calls "Lee," collaborate on various projects with the CIA and FBI.

But their intelligence activities put a target on their backs. They narrowly escape four assassination attempts.

Leonardo Murphy is a breathtakingly fast coming-of-age thriller about one of the most fascinating characters you will ever meet in literature. Instantly, you are shoulder to shoulder with the world's most amazing genius.

"Finally, a believable super hero comes to life! Peaks and valleys of horrific actions are neatly juxtaposed against comic relief. The humor, ranging between the poles of mild to downright hysterical, will surely tickle your funny bone. The frequent use of the protagonist's favorite word (26 matches found throughout), which I won't divulge, would ordinarily belabor one's prose, save when Leonardo employs the term. As a matter of fact, the story concludes with that very word, but rather endearingly. No, I did not ruin the ending for you folks. You'll see." – Robert Banfelder

The Pineaire Incident – Book 4 of the Harry and Meg Series
https://amzn.to/2VXQ2lp

One hundred gigantic fast submarines suddenly appear in the ocean.

President Harry Fenton and his First Lady, Meg are shocked by the event, as are all the leaders of the world.

Where are the submarines from? What do they want? What are their intentions?

Six Russian submarines attack one of the mystery subs. All six Russian subs are destroyed in two minutes.

President Fenton, along with Meg, reaches out to contact the leader of the strange fleet. They are amazed to discover that the subs are from another planet, Planet Pineaire.

But they're pleased to find out that the Pinearians came in peace, and bring with them an amazing gift, a new type of fuel that can revolutionize life on earth.

Get ready for an interplanetary thrill ride. *The Pinaire Incident* is Book 4 of the Harry and Meg series.

"Right at the beginning, we learn that 100 giant submarines are discovered with no idea how they could all suddenly appear. Being familiar with Harry & Meg, I immediately presumed they must have Time Traveled from some future time. Uh Oh, I almost gave away an important detail. You should already know that Harry and Meg are President and First Lady having recently defeated a small rogue nation that destroyed the Cruise Ship industry and nearly took over the world's Shipping Industry. You might think peaceful times are ahead when abruptly, 100 of these 1,800 foot long submarines appear. Five Stars" – The Holey One

Puzzles Book 1 – A Detective Love Story
https://amzn.to/2MI6TEo

Veteran police detectives Bobbie Nelson and Bob Lawton are partnered. They're both concerned that they may not get along. They're both highly skilled and love their work—They love to solve puzzles. They soon learn that they don't just love their jobs, they love each other. *Puzzles* is an action-packed police thriller wrapped around a sweet romance.

Bobbie and Bob are two of the most exciting and likeable characters you will find in literature.

"This book should be kept out of the hands of crooks, criminals, terrorists, and any others planning to do evil. There are so many techniques utilized by skilled detectives that are revealed that this book could be used as a training guide by the Bad Guys. Even so, the reality is that fundamental police work is what solves most crimes. Gathering and evaluating massive amounts of data and looking for patterns or repeating details is what our two main characters excel at." – The Holey One

"Russell Moran has done it again with Puzzles: A Detective Love Story. Each case builds upon earlier ones, with the BBs fine-tuning their puzzle-solving techniques to such a degree it's not long before the FBI and CIA reach out them to piece together more complicated scenarios impacting on society. Russell has created an easy-to-read and fast-paced story, which will keep you turning the pages late into the evening to find out what happens next. I can't wait for the next book in the series!" – R. J. Krzak

Puzzles, Book 2 – A Detective Love Story
https://amzn.to/3bmiqEh

The further adventures of Detectives Bob Lawton and Bobbie Nelson, now married.

About the Author

In addition to the 19 novels discussed above, I also published five nonfiction books: *Justice in America: How it Works – How it Fails; The APT Principle: The Business Plan That You Carry in Your Head; Boating Basics: The Boattalk Book of Boating Tips; If You're Injured: A Consumer Guide to Personal Injury Law; How to Create More Time*. My latest nonfiction book is *The Novel - A Writer's Guide - Discover the Joy of Writing Fiction* published in November 2018.

I'm a lawyer and a veteran of the United States Navy. I live on Long Island, New York, with my wife and editor, Lynda, a Shih-Tzu named Sammie, and a Golden Retriever named Maggie. Maggie plays an important cameo role in the book.

A Personal Request

I hope you enjoyed reading *The Long Island Project* as much as I enjoyed writing it. Bob and Bobbie are now two of my favorite characters. I think of them as old friends. You will be seeing more of them in future books.

Please consider leaving a brief review on amazon.com. It doesn't need to be lengthy or elaborate, just your thoughts on the characters, the scenes, and the story. Book reviews are the lifeblood of an author.